Under the cover, he pulled her into his arms.

"Now!" he said.

Pleasure and relief went through her. She had wanted this so much, and now everything in her yearned toward him. His kiss was everything she'd wanted since their meeting. Nothing else in her life had been like it. Nothing else ever would be.

"What have you done to me?" he growled. "Why can't I stop you doing it?"

Lysandros felt as if he were awaking from a dream, or sinking into one. He wasn't sure which. Her plea of "Kiss me" was entrancing, yet something deep inside him was drawing away. He tried to fight it. He wanted her, but so much that it alarmed him.

Impulse had made him call her tonight. Impulse had made him drag her away from their unwanted companions. Impulse, the thing he'd battled for years, was turning him into its creature.

Her creature! The words screamed at him. A puppet dancing on the end of her chain. And she knew it.

"What is it?" she asked, feeling him draw away.

"This place is very public. I think we should both— go home."

She stared at him, trying to believe what he was doing, feeling the anger rise within her. He was telling her the magic was over. He'd banished it by an act of will, proving that his control was still strong, although he'd brought her to the edge of losing hers.

LUCY GORDON cut her writing teeth on magazine journalism, interviewing many of the world's most interesting men, including Warren Beatty, Richard Chamberlain, Roger Moore, Sir Alec Guinness and Sir John Gielgud. She has also camped out with lions in Africa, and had many other unusual experiences, which have often provided the background for her books. She is married to a Venetian, whom she met while on holiday in Venice. They got engaged within two days.

Two of her books have won a Romance Writers of America RITA® Award—*Song of the Lorelei* in 1990 and *His Brother's Child* in 1998, in the Best Traditional Romance category. You can visit her Web site at www.lucy-gordon.com.

THE GREEK TYCOON'S ACHILLES HEEL
LUCY GORDON

~ The Greek Tycoons ~

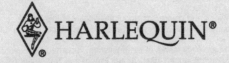

TORONTO • NEW YORK • LONDON
AMSTERDAM • PARIS • SYDNEY • HAMBURG
STOCKHOLM • ATHENS • TOKYO • MILAN • MADRID
PRAGUE • WARSAW • BUDAPEST • AUCKLAND

Recycling programs
for this product may
not exist in your area.

ISBN-13: 978-0-373-52769-4

THE GREEK TYCOON'S ACHILLES HEEL

First North American Publication 2010.

Copyright © 2010 by Lucy Gordon.

THE GREEK TYCOON'S
ACHILLES HEEL

PROLOGUE

THE lights of the Las Vegas Strip gleamed and glittered up into the night sky. Down below, the hotels and casinos rioted with life and money but the Palace Athena outshone them all.

In the six months since its opening it had gained a reputation for being more lavish than its competitors, and today it had put the seal on its success by hosting the wedding of the beautiful, glamorous film star, Estelle Radnor.

The owner of the Palace, no fool, had gained the prestige of staging her wedding by offering everything for free, and the gorgeous Estelle, also no fool where money was concerned, whatever might be said of her taste in men, had seized the offer.

The wedding party finished up in the casino, where the bride was photographed throwing dice, embracing her groom, throwing more dice, slipping an arm around the shoulders of a thin, nondescript young girl, then throwing more dice. The owner watched it all with satisfaction, before turning to a young man who stood regarding the performance sardonically.

'Achilles, my friend—'

'I've told you before, don't call me that.'

'But your name has brought me such good luck. Your excellent advice on how to make this place convincingly Greek—'

'None of which you've taken.'

'Well, my customers *believe* it's Greek and that's what matters.'

'Of course, appearance is everything and what else counts?' the young man murmured.

'You're gloomy tonight. Is it the wedding? Do you envy them?'

'Achilles' turned on him with swift ferocity. 'Don't talk nonsense!' he snapped. 'All I feel is boredom and disgust.'

'Have things gone badly for you?'

A shrug. 'I've lost a million. Before the night's out I'll probably lose another. So what?'

'Come and join the party.'

'I haven't been invited.'

'You think they're going to turn away the son of the wealthiest man in Greece?'

'They're not going to get the chance. Leave me and get back to your guests.'

He strolled away, a lean, isolated figure, followed by two pairs of eyes, one belonging to the man he'd just left, the other to the awkward-looking teenager the bride had earlier embraced. Keeping close to the wall, so as not to be noticed, she slipped away and took the elevator to the fifty-second floor, where she could observe the Strip.

Here, both the walls and the roof were thick glass, allowing visitors to look out in safety. Outside ran a ledge which she guessed was there for workmen and window cleaners, but inaccessible to customers unless they knew the code to tap into the lock.

She was staring down, transfixed, when a slight noise made her turn and see the young man from downstairs. Moving quietly into the shadows, she watched, unnoticed, as he came to stand nearby, gazing down a thousand feet at the dazzling, distant world beneath.

Up here there were only a few lamps, so that customers could look out through the glass. She had a curious view of his face, lit from below by a glow that shifted and changed colour. His features were lean and clean-cut, their slight sharpness emphasised by the angle. It was the face of a very young man, little more than a boy, yet it held a weariness—even a despair—that suggested a crushing burden.

Then he did something that terrified her, reaching out to the code box and tapping in a number, making a pane of glass slide back so that there was nothing but air between him and a thousand foot drop. Petra's sharp gasp made him turn his head.

'What are you doing there?' he snapped. 'Are you spying on me?'

'Of course not. Come back in, please,' she begged. 'Don't do it.'

He stepped back into comparative safety, but remained near the gap.

'What the hell do you mean, "don't do it"?' he snapped. 'I wasn't going to *do* anything. I wanted some air.'

'But it's dangerous. You could fall by accident.'

'I know what I'm doing. Go away and let me be.'

'No,' she said defiantly. 'I have as much right to take the air as you. Is it nice out there?'

'What?'

Moving so fast that she took him by surprise, she slipped past him and out onto the ledge. At once the wind attacked her so that she had to reach out and found him grasping her.

'You stupid woman!' he shouted. 'I'm not the only one who can have an accident. Do you want to die?'

'Do you?'

'Come inside.'

He yanked her back in, stopping short in surprise when he saw her face.

'Didn't I see you downstairs?'

'Yes, I was in the Zeus Room,' she said, naming the casino. 'I like watching people. That place is very cleverly named.'

'You know what Zeus means, then?' he asked, drawing her away to where they could sit down.

'He was the King of the Greek gods,' she said, 'looking down on the world from his home on the top of Mount Olympus, master of all he surveyed. That must be how the gamblers feel when they start playing, but the poor idiots soon learn differently. Did you lose much?'

He shrugged. 'A million. I stopped counting after a while. What are you doing in a casino, anyway? You can't be more than fifteen.'

'I'm seventeen and I'm…one of the bridal party.'

'That's right,' he said, seeming not to notice the way she'd checked herself at the last moment. 'I saw her embracing you for the camera. Are you a bridesmaid?'

She regarded him cynically. 'Do I look like a bridesmaid?' she demanded, indicating her attire, which was clearly expensive but not glamorous.

'Well—'

'I don't really belong in front of the cameras, not with that lot.'

She spoke with a wry lack of self-pity that was attractive. Looking at her more closely, he saw that she wore no make-up, her hair was cut efficiently short, and she'd made no attempt to enhance her appearance.

'And your name is—?' he queried.

'Petra. And you're Achilles. No?' The last word was a response to his scowl.

'My name is Lysandros Demetriou. My mother wanted to call me Achilles, but my father thought she was being sentimental. In the end they compromised, and Achilles became my second name.'

'But that man downstairs called you by it.'

'It's important to him that I'm Greek because this place is built on the idea of Greekness.'

To his delight she gave a cheeky giggle. 'They're all potty.'

They took stock of each other. He was as handsome as she'd first sensed, with clean cut features, deep set eyes and an air of pride that came with a lifetime of having his own way. But there was also a darkness and a brooding intensity that seemed strange in this background. Young men in Las Vegas hunted in packs, savouring every experience. This one hid away, treasuring his solitude as though the world was an enemy. And something had driven him to take the air in a place full of danger.

'Demetriou Shipbuilding?' she asked.

'That's the one.'

'The most powerful firm in Greece.' She said it as though reciting a lesson. 'What they don't want isn't worth having. What they don't acquire today they'll acquire tomorrow. If anyone dares to refuse them, they wait in the shadows until the right moment to pounce.'

He grunted. 'Something like that.'

'Or maybe you'll just turn the Furies onto them?'

She meant the three Greek goddesses of wrath and vengeance, with hair made of snakes and eyes that dripped blood, who hounded their victims without mercy.

'Do you have to be melodramatic?' he demanded.

'In this "pretend" Greek place I can't help it. Anyway, why aren't you in Athens grinding your enemies to dust?'

'I've done with all that,' he said harshly. 'They can get on without me.'

'Ah, this is the bit where you sulk.'

'*What?*'

'During the Trojan war Achilles was in love with this girl. She actually came from the other side, and was his prisoner, but they made him give her back, so he withdrew from the battle and sulked in his tent. But in the end he came out and started fighting again. Only he ended up dead. As you could have done on that ledge.'

'I told you I wasn't planning to die, although frankly it doesn't seem important one way or the other. I'll take what comes.'

'Did she do something very cruel?' Petra asked gently.

In the dim light she could barely see the look he turned on her, but she sensed that it was terrible. His eyes were harsh and cold in the gloom, warning her that she'd trespassed on sacred ground.

'Stop now!' howled the Furies. 'Run for your life before he strikes you dead.'

But that wasn't her way.

'She?' he asked in a voice that warned her.

She laid a gentle hand on his arm, whispering, 'I'm sorry. Shouldn't I have said that?'

He rose sharply and strode back to the gap in the glass wall and stood gazing out into the night. She followed cautiously.

'She made me trust her,' he whispered.

'But sometimes it's right to trust.'

'No,' he insisted. 'Nobody is ever as good as you think they are, and sooner or later the truth is always there. The more you trust someone, the worse it is when they betray you. Better to have no illusions, and be strong.'

'But that would be terrible, never to believe in anything, never to love or hope, never be really happy—'

'Never to be wretched,' he said harshly.

'Never to be alive,' she said with gentle urgency. 'It would be a living death, can't you see that? You'd escape suffering, but you'd also lose everything that makes life worth living.'

'Not everything. There's power. You'd gain that if you did without the other things. They're only weaknesses.'

'No,' she said, almost violently. 'You mustn't give in to that way of thinking or you'll ruin your life.'

'And what do you know about it?' he demanded, angry now. 'You're a child. Has anyone ever made you want to smash things and keep on smashing until nothing is left alive—including yourself?'

'But what do you gain by destroying yourself inside?' she demanded.

'I'll tell you what you gain. You don't become—like this.' He jabbed a finger at his heart.

She didn't have to ask what he meant. Young as he was, he lived on the edge of disaster, and it would take very little to push him over. That was why he dared to stand here, defying the fates to do their worst.

Pity and terror almost overwhelmed her. Part of her wanted to run for her life, get far, far away from this creature who might become a monster if something didn't intervene. But the other part wanted to stay and be the one to rescue him.

Suddenly, without warning, he did the thing that decided her, something terrible and wonderful in the same moment. Lowering his head, he let it fall against her shoulder, raised it, dropped it again, and again and again. It was like watching a man bang his head against a brick wall, hopelessly, robotically.

Appalled, she threw her arms around him and clutched a restraining hand over his head, forcing him to be still. His despair seemed to reach out to her, imploring her comfort, saying that only she could give it to him. To be needed so desperately was a new experience for her and, even in the midst of her dismay, she knew a kind of delight.

Over his shoulder she could see the drop, with nothing to protect him from it. Nothing but herself. She gripped him tight, silently offering him all she could. He didn't resist, but now his head rested on her shoulder as though the strength had drained out of him.

When she drew back to see his face the bitter anguish had gone, leaving it sad and resigned, as though he'd found a kind of peace, albeit a bleak and despairing peace.

At last Lysandros gave her a faint smile, feeling deep within him a desire to protect her as she had tried to protect him. There was still good in the world. It was here in this girl, too innocent to understand the danger she ran just by being here with him. In the end she would be sullied and spoiled like the rest.

But not tonight. He wouldn't allow it.

He tapped a number into the code pad and the glass panel closed.

'Let's go,' he said, leading her away from the roof and down into the hotel.

Outside her door he said, 'Go inside, go to bed, don't open this door to anyone.'

'What are you going to do?'

'I'm going to lose a lot more money. After that—I'm going to do some thinking.'

He hadn't meant to say the last words.

'Goodnight, Achilles.'

'Goodnight.'

He hadn't intended what he did next either, but on impulse he leaned down and kissed her mouth gently.

'Go in,' he said. 'And lock your door.'

She nodded and slipped inside. After a moment he heard the key turn.

He returned to the tables, resigned to further losses, but mysteriously his luck turned. In an hour he'd recovered every penny. In another hour he'd doubled it.

So that was who she was, a good luck charm, sent to cast her spell and change his fortunes. He only hoped he'd also done something for her, but he would probably never know. They would never meet again.

He was wrong. They did meet again.

But not for fifteen years.

CHAPTER ONE

THE Villa Demetriou stood on the outskirts of Athens on raised ground, from which the family had always been able to survey the domain they considered theirs. Until now the only thing that could rival them had been the Parthenon, the great classical temple built more than two thousand years before, high on the Acropolis, far away across the city and just visible.

Recently a new rival had sprung up, a fake Parthenon, created by Homer Lukas, the one man in Greece who would have ventured to challenge either the Demetriou family or the ancient gods who protected the true temple. But Homer was in love, and naturally wished to impress his bride on their wedding day.

On that spring morning Lysandros Demetriou stood in the doorway of his villa, looking out across Athens, irritated by having to waste his time at a wedding when he had so many really important things to deal with.

A sound behind him made him turn to see the entrance of Stavros, an old friend of his late father, who lived just outside the city. He was white-haired and far too thin, the result of a lifetime of self-indulgence.

'I'm on my way to the wedding,' he said. 'I called in to see if you fancied a lift.'

'Thank you, that would be useful,' Lysandros said coolly. 'If I arrive early it won't give too much offence if I leave early.'

Stavros gave a crack of laughter. 'You're not sentimental about weddings.'

'It's not a wedding, it's an exhibition,' he said sardonically. 'Homer Lukas has acquired a film star wife and is flaunting her to the world. The world will offer him good wishes and call him names behind his back. My own wish for him is that Estelle Radnor will make a fool of him. With any luck, she will.

'Why did she have to come to Athens to get married, anyway? Why not make do with a false Greek setting, like that other time?'

'Because the name of Homer Lukas is synonymous with Greek shipbuilding,' Stavros said, adding quickly, 'after yourself, of course.'

For years the companies of Demetriou and Lukas had stood head and shoulders above all others in Greece, or even in the world, some reverently claimed.

They were opponents, foes, even outright enemies, but enemies who presented a civilised veneer to outsiders because it was profitable to do so.

'I suppose it might be a real love-match,' Stavros observed cynically.

Lysandros raised his eyebrows. 'A real—? How many times has she been married? Six, seven?'

'You should know. Weren't you a guest at one of the previous weddings, years ago?'

'Not a guest. I just happened to be in the Las Vegas hotel where it was held and watched some of the shenanigans from a safe distance. And I returned to Greece the next day.'

'Yes, I remember that. Your father was very puzzled— pleased, but puzzled. Apparently you'd told him you wanted nothing more to do with the business now or ever again. You vanished for two years, but suddenly, out of the blue, you just walked in the door and said you were ready to go to work. He was even afraid you wouldn't be up to it after…well…'

He fell silent, alarmed by the grim look that had come over Lysandros's face.

'Quite,' he said in a quiet voice that was more frightening than a shout. 'Well, it's a long time ago. The past is over.'

'Yes, and your father said that all his fears were groundless because when you returned you were different, a tiger who terrified everyone. He was so proud.'

'Well, let's hope I terrify Homer Lukas. Otherwise I'm losing my touch.'

'Perhaps you should be scared,' Stavros said. 'Such threats he's been uttering since you recently bilked him and his son of billions. *Stole* billions, according to him.'

'I didn't steal anything, I merely offered the client a better deal,' Lysandros said indifferently.

'But it was at the last minute,' Stavros recalled. 'Apparently they were all assembled to sign the contracts, and the client had actually lifted the pen when his phone rang and it was you, giving him some information that you could only have acquired "by disgraceful means".'

'Not as disgraceful as all that,' Lysandros observed with a shrug. 'I've done worse, I'm glad to say.'

'And that was that,' Stavros resumed. 'The man put the pen down, cancelled the deal and walked out straight into your car, waiting outside. Rumour says Homer promised the gods on Olympus splendid offerings if only they would punish you.'

'But I've remained unpunished, so perhaps the gods weren't listening. They say he even uttered a curse over my wedding invitation. I hope he did.'

'You're really not taking anyone with you?'

Lysandros made a non-committal reply. He attended many weddings as a duty, sometimes with companions but never with one woman. It would interest the press too much, and send out misleading signals to the lady herself, which could cause him serious inconvenience.

'Right, let's get going,' Stavros said.

'I'm afraid I'll have to catch you up later,' Lysandros excused himself.

'But you just said you'd go with me—'

'Yes, but I've suddenly remembered something I must do first. Goodbye.'

There was a finality in the last word that Stavros dared not challenge.

His car was waiting downstairs. In the back sat his wife, who'd refused to come in with him on the grounds that she hated the desolate house that seemed to suit Lysandros so perfectly.

'How can he bear to live in that vast, silent place with no family and only servants for company?' she'd demanded more than once. 'It makes me shiver. And that's not the only thing about Lysandros that makes me shiver.'

In that, she knew she was not alone. Most of Athens would have agreed. Now, when Stavros had described the conversation, she said, 'Why did he change his mind about coming with us?'

'My fault. I stupidly mentioned the past, and he froze. It's almost eerie the way he's blotted that time out as though it never happened, yet it drives everything he does. Look at what happened just now. One minute he was fine, the next he couldn't get rid of me fast enough.'

'I wonder why he's really going to leave early.'

'He'll probably pass the time with a floozy.'

'If you mean—' she said a name, 'she's hardly a floozy. Her husband's one of the most influential men on the—'

'Which makes her a high class floozy, and she's keeping

her distance now because her husband has put his foot down. Rumours reached him.'

'He probably knew all the time,' his wife said cynically. 'There are men in this city who don't mind their women sleeping with Lysandros.'

Stavros nodded. 'Yes, but I gather she became too "emotional", started expecting too much, so he dropped the husband a hint to rein her in if he knew what was good for him.'

'Surely even Lysandros wouldn't be so cruel, so cold-blooded—'

'That's exactly what he is, and in our hearts we all know it,' Stavros said flatly.

'I wonder about *his* heart,' she mused.

'He doesn't have one, which is why he keeps people at a distance.'

As the car turned out of the gate Stavros couldn't resist looking back to the house. Lysandros stood there at the window, watching the world with a brooding air, as though it was his personal property and he had yet to decide how to manage it.

He remained there until the car had vanished through the gates, then turned back into the room, trying to clear his mind. The conversation had disturbed him and that must be quickly remedied. Luckily an urgent call came through from his manager at the port of Piraeus, to say that they were threatened with union trouble. Lysandros gave him a series of curt orders and promised to be there the next day.

Today he would attend Homer Lukas's wedding as an honoured guest. He would shake his rival's hand, show honour to the bride, and the watching crowds would sigh with disappointment not to see them at each other's throats, personally as well as professionally.

Now, more than ever, his father's advice rang in his head. *'Never, never let them know what you're thinking.'*

He'd learned that lesson well and, with its aid, he would spend today with a smile on his face, concealing the hatred that consumed him.

At last it was time for his chauffeur to take him to the Lukas estate. Soon he could see Homer's 'Parthenon', in which the wedding was to take place, and it loomed up high, proclaiming the residence of a wealthy and influential man.

A fake, he thought grimly. No more authentic than the other 'Greek setting' in Las Vegas.

His thoughts went back to a time that felt like another world and through his mind danced the girl on the roof, skinny, ordinary, yet with an outspoken innocence that had both exasperated and charmed him. And at the last moment, when she'd opened her arms to him, offering a comfort he'd found nowhere else in the world and he'd almost—

He slammed his mind shut. It was the only way to deal with weakness.

He wondered how she'd come to be one of the wedding party; probably the daughter of one of Estelle Radnor's numerous secretaries.

She might be here today, but it was probably better not to meet again after so long. Time was never kind. The years would have turned her into a dull wife with several children and a faithless husband. Where once she had sparkled, now she would probably seethe.

Nor had he himself been improved by time, he knew. A heaviness had settled over him, different from the raging grief that had possessed him in those days. That had been a matter of the heart and he'd dealt with it suitably, setting it aside, focusing on his head, where all sensible action took place.

He'd done what was right and wise, yet he had an uneasy feeling that if he met her now she would look right through him—and disapprove.

At last they arrived. As he got out of his car and looked around he had to admit that Homer had spent money to great effect. The great temple to the goddess Athena had been re-created much as the original must have looked when it was new. The building was about seventy metres by thirty, the roof held aloft by elegant columns. Marvellous statues abounded, but the greatest of all was the forty-foot statue of Athena, which had mysteriously developed the face of Estelle Radnor.

He grimaced, wondering how long it would be before he could decently depart.

But, before he could start his social duties, his cellphone shrilled. It was a text message.

I'm sorry about what I said. I was upset. You seemed to be pulling away when we'd been growing so close. Please call me.

It was signed only with an initial. He immediately texted back.

No need to be sorry. You were right to break it off. Forgive me for upsetting you.

Hopefully that would be an end to it, but after a moment another text came through.

I don't want to break off. I really didn't mean all those things. Will I see you at the wedding? We could talk there.

This time it was signed with her name. He responded.

We always knew it couldn't last. We can't talk. I don't wish to subject you to gossip.

The answer came in seconds.

I don't care about gossip. I love you.

Madness seemed to have come over her, for now she'd stepped up the intensity, signing *your own forever*, followed by her name. His response was brief.

Please accept my good wishes for the future. Make sure you delete texts from your phone. Goodbye.

After that he switched off. In every way. To silence a

machine was easy. It was the switching off of the heart and mind that took skill, but it was one he'd acquired with practice, sharpening it to perfection until he would have guaranteed it against every female in the world.

Except perhaps one.

But he would never meet her again.

Unless he was very unlucky.

Or very lucky.

'You look *gorgeous*!'

Petra Radnor laughed aside the fervent compliment from Nikator Lukas.

'Thank you, brother dear,' she said.

'Don't call me that. I'm not your brother.'

'You will be in a couple of hours, when your father has married my mother.'

'Stepbrother at most. We won't be related by blood and I can yearn after you if I want to.'

'No, I think you'll be the brother I've always wanted. My *kid* brother.'

'Kid, nothing! I'm older than you.'

It was true. He was thirty-seven to her thirty-two, but there was something about him that suggested a kid; not just the boyish lines of his face but a lingering immaturity that would probably be there all his life.

Petra liked him well enough, except for his black moods that seemed to come from nowhere, although they also vanished quickly.

He admired her extravagantly, and she justified his admiration. The gaunt figure of her teen years had blossomed, although she would always be naturally slender.

She was attractive but not beautiful, certainly not as the word was understood among her mother's film-land friends.

She had a vivid personality that gleamed from her eyes and a humour that was never long suppressed. But the true effect was often discovered only after she'd departed, when she lingered in the mind.

To divert Nikator's attention, she turned the conversation to Debra, the starlet who would be his official companion.

'You two look wonderful together,' she said. 'Everyone will say what a lucky man you are.'

'I'd rather go with you,' he sighed.

'Oh, stop it! After all the trouble Estelle took to fix you up with her, you should be grateful.'

'Debra's gorgeous,' he conceded. 'At least Demetriou won't have anything to match her.'

'Demetriou? Do you mean Lysandros Demetriou?' Petra asked, suddenly concentrating on a button. '*The* Lysandros Demetriou?'

'There's no need to say it like that, as though he was important,' Nikator said at once.

'He certainly seems to be. Didn't he—?'

'Never mind that. He probably won't have a woman on his arm.'

'I've heard he has quite a reputation with women.'

'True. But he never takes them out in public. Too much hassle, I guess. To him they're disposable. I'll tell you this, half the women who come here today will have been in his bed.'

'You really hate him, don't you?' she asked curiously.

'Years ago he was involved with a girl from this family, but he ill-treated her.'

'How?'

'I don't know the details. Nobody does.'

'Then maybe she ill-treated him,' Petra suggested. 'And he reacted badly because he was disillusioned.'

He glared at her. 'Why would you think that?'

'I don't know,' she said, suddenly confused. A voice had whispered mysteriously in her mind, but she couldn't quite make out the words. It came from long ago, and haunted her across the years. If only—

She tried to listen but now there was only silence.

'She fled, and later we heard that she was dead,' Nikator continued. 'It was years ago, but he knew how to put the knife in, even then. Be warned. When he knows you're connected with this family he'll try to seduce you, just to show us that he can do it.'

'Seduce?' she echoed with hilarity. 'What do you think I am—some helpless maiden? After all this time around the film industry I've learned to be safely cynical, I promise you. I've even been known to do a bit of "seducing" myself.'

His eyes gleamed and he reached out hopeful hands. 'Ah, in that case—'

'Be off,' she told him firmly. 'It's time you left to collect Debra.'

He dashed away, much to her relief. There were aspects of Nikki that were worrying, but that must wait. This was supposed to be a happy day.

She checked her camera. There would be an army of professional photographers here today, but Estelle, as she always called her mother, had asked her to take some intimate family pictures.

She took one last look in the mirror, then frowned at what she saw. As Nikator had said, she looked gorgeous, but what might be right for other women wasn't right for Estelle Radnor's daughter. This was the bride's big day, and she alone must occupy the spotlight.

'Something a little more restrained, I think,' Petra murmured.

She found a darker dress, plainer, more puritanical. Then she swept her luxuriant hair back into a bun and studied herself again.

'That's better. Nobody will look at me now.'

She'd grown up making these adjustments to her mother's ego. It was no longer a big deal. She was fond of Estelle, but the centre of her life was elsewhere.

The bride had already moved into the great mansion, and now occupied the suite belonging to the mistress of the house. Petra hurried along to say a last encouraging word before it was time to start.

That was when things went wrong.

Estelle screamed when she saw her daughter.

'Darling, what are you thinking of to dress like that? You look like a Victorian governess.'

Petra, who was used to her mother's way of putting things, didn't take offence. She knew by now that it was pointless.

'I thought I'd keep it plain,' she said. 'You're the one they'll be looking at. And you look absolutely wonderful. You'll be the most beautiful bride ever.'

'But people know you're *my* daughter,' Estella moaned. 'If you go out there looking middle-aged, what will they say about *me*?'

'Perhaps you could pretend I'm not your daughter,' Petra said with wry good humour.

'It's too late for that. They already know. You've got to look young and innocent or they'll wonder how old *I* am. Really, darling, you might try to do *me* credit.'

'I'm sorry. Shall I go and change?'

'Yes, do it quickly. And take your hair down.'

'All right, I'll change. Have a wonderful day.'

She kissed her mother and felt herself embraced as warmly as though there'd never been an argument. Which, in a sense, was true. Having got her own way, Estelle had forgotten it had ever happened.

As she left the room Petra was smiling, thinking it lucky

that she had a sense of humour. Thirty-two years as Estelle Radnor's daughter had had certain advantages, but they had also demanded reserves of patience.

Back in her room, she reversed the changes, donning the elegantly simple blue silk dress she'd worn before and brushing her hair free so that it fell gloriously about her shoulders. Then she went out into the grounds where the crowds were gathering and plunged into introductions. She smiled and said the right things, but part of her attention was elsewhere, scanning the men to see if Lysandros Demetriou had arrived.

The hour they had spent together, long ago, now felt like a dream, but he'd always held her interest. She'd followed his career as far as she could, gathering the sparse details of his life that seeped out. He was unmarried and, since his father's death had made him the boss of Demetriou Shipbuilding, he lived alone. That was all the world was allowed to know.

Occasionally she saw a photograph that she could just identify as the man she'd met in Las Vegas. These days his face looked fearsome, but now another face came into her mind, a naïve, disillusioned young lover, tortured out of his mind, crying, 'She made me trust her,' as though that was the worst crime in the world.

The recent pictures showed a man on whom harshness had settled early. It was hard to realise that he was the same person who'd clung to her on that high roof, seeking refuge, not from the physical danger he'd freely courted, but from the demons that howled in his head.

What had become of that need and despair? Had he yielded to the desire to destroy everything, including his own heart?

What would he say to her if they met now?

Petra was no green girl. Nor was she a prude. In the years since then she'd been married, divorced, and enjoyed male company to the full. But that encounter, short but searingly intense, lived in her mind, her heart and her senses. The awareness of an overwhelming presence was with her still, and so was the disappointment she'd felt when he'd parted from her with only the lightest touch of the lips.

Now the thought of meeting Lysandros Demetriou again gave her a frisson of pleasurable curiosity and excitement. But strangely there was also a touch of nervousness. He'd loomed so large in her imagination that she feared lest the reality disappoint her.

Then she saw him.

She was standing on the slope, watching the advancing crowd, and even among so many it was easy to discern him. It wasn't just that he was taller than most men; it was the same intense quality that had struck her so forcefully the first time, and which now seemed to sing over the distance.

The pictures hadn't done him justice, she realised. The boy had grown into a handsome man whose stern features, full of pride and aloofness, would have drawn eyes anywhere. In Las Vegas she'd seen him mostly in poor light. Now she could make out that his eyes were dark and deep-set, as though even there he was holding part of himself back.

Nikator had said no woman would be with him, and that was true. Lysandros Demetriou walked alone. Even in that milling crowd he gave the impression that nobody could get anywhere near him. Occasionally someone tried to claim his attention. He replied briefly and passed on.

The photographer in Petra smiled. Here was a man whose picture would be worth taking, and if that displeased him at first he would surely forgive her, for the sake of their old acquaintance.

She took a picture, then another. Smiling, she began to walk down until she was only a few feet in front of him. He glanced up, noticed the camera and scowled.

'Put that away,' he said.

'But—'

'And get out of my sight.'

Before she could speak again he'd passed on. Petra was left alone, her smile fading as she realised that he'd looked right through her without a hint of recognition.

There was nothing to do but move on with the crowd and take her place in the temple. She tried to shrug and reason with herself. So he hadn't recognised her! So what? It had been years ago and she'd changed a lot.

But, she thought wryly, she could dismiss any fantasies about memories reaching over time. Instead, it might be the chance to have a little fun.

Yes, fun would be good. Fun would punish him!

The music started as the bride made her entrance, magnificently attired in fawn satin, looking nowhere near fifty, her true age.

Petra joined the other photographers, and forgot everything except what she was meant to be doing. It was an ability that had carried her through some difficult times in her life.

Lysandros was seated in the front row. He frowned at her as if trying to work something out, then turned his attention to the ceremony.

The vows were spoken in Greek. The bride had learned her part well, but there was just one moment when she hesitated. Quickly, Petra moved beside her, murmured something in Greek and stepped back. Lysandros, watching, frowned again.

Then the bride and groom were moving slowly away, smiling at the crowd, two wealthy, powerful people, revelling in having acquired each other. Everyone began to leave the temple.

'Lysandros, my friend, how good to see you.'

He turned and saw Nikator advancing on him, arms outstretched as though welcoming a long-lost friend. Assuming a smile, he returned the greeting. With a flourish Nikator introduced his companion, Debra Farley. Lysandros acted suitably impressed. This continued until everyone felt that enough time had elapsed, and then the couple moved on.

Lysandros took a long breath of relief at having got that out of the way.

A slight choke made him turn and see the young woman with the luscious fair hair. She was laughing as though he'd just performed for her entertainment, and he was suddenly gripped by a rising tension, neither pleasure nor pain but a mysterious combination of both, as though the world had shifted on its axis and nothing would ever be the same again.

CHAPTER TWO

'You did that very convincingly,' Petra said. 'You should get an Oscar.'

She'd spoken in Greek and he replied in the same language.

'I wasn't as convincing as all that if you saw through me.'

'Oh, I automatically disbelieve everyone,' she said in a teasing voice. 'It saves a lot of time.'

He gave a polite smile. 'How wise. You're used to this kind of event, then? Do you work for Homer?' He indicated her camera.

'No, I've only recently met him.'

'What do you think of him?'

'I've never seen a man so in love.' She shook her head, as if suggesting that this passed all understanding.

'Yes, it's a pity,' he said.

'What do you mean?'

'You don't think the bride's in love with him, surely? To her, he's a decoration to flaunt in her buttonhole, in addition to the diamonds he's showered on her. The best of her career is over so she scoops him up to put on her mantelpiece. It almost makes me feel sorry for him, and I never thought I'd say that.'

'But that means someone has brought him low at last,' she

pointed out. 'You should be grateful to her. Think how much easier you'll find it to defeat him in future.'

She was regarding him with her head on one side and an air of detached amusement, as though he was an interesting specimen laid out for her entertainment. A sudden frisson went through him. He didn't understand why, and yet—

'I think I can manage that without help,' he observed.

'Now, there's a thought,' she said, apparently much struck. 'Have you noticed how weddings bring out the worst in people? I'm sure you aren't usually as cynical and grumpy as now.'

This was sheer impertinence, but instead of brushing her aside he felt an unusual inclination to spar with her.

'Certainly not,' he said. 'I'm usually worse.'

'Impossible.'

'Anyone who knows me will tell you that this is my "sweetness and light" mood.'

'I don't believe it. Instinct tells me that you're a softie at heart. People cry on your shoulder, children flock to you, those in trouble turn to you first.'

'I've done nothing to deserve that,' he assured her fervently.

The crowd was swirling around them, forcing them to move aside. As they left the temple, Lysandros observed, 'I'm surprised Homer settled for an imitation Parthenon.'

'Oh, he wanted the original,' she agreed, 'but between you and me—' she lowered her voice dramatically '—it didn't quite measure up to his standards, and he felt he could do better. So he built this to show them how it ought to have been done.'

Before he could stop himself he gave a crack of laughter and several people stared at the sight of this famously dour man actually enjoying a joke. A society journalist passing by stared, then made a hasty note.

She responded to his laughter with more of her own. He led her to where the drinks were being served and presented her with a glass of champagne, feeling that, just for once, it was good to be light-hearted. She had the power of making tension vanish, even if only briefly.

The tables for the wedding feast were outside in the sun. The guests were taking their places, preparing for the moment when the newly married couple would appear.

'I'll be back in a moment,' she said.

'Just a minute. You haven't told me who you are.'

She glanced back, regarding him with a curious smile. 'No, I haven't, have I? Perhaps I thought there would be no need. I'll see you later.'

Briefly she raised her champagne glass to him before hurrying away.

'You're a sly devil,' said a deep voice behind him.

A large bearded man stood there and with pleasure Lysandros recognised an old ally.

'Georgios,' he exclaimed. 'I might have known you'd be where there was the best food.'

'The best food, the best wine, the best women. Well, you've found that for yourself.' He indicated the young woman's retreating figure.

'She's charming,' Lysandros said with a slight reserve. He didn't choose to discuss her.

'Oh, don't worry, I'll back off. I don't aspire to Estelle Radnor's daughter.'

Lysandros tensed. 'What are you talking about?'

'I don't blame you for wanting to keep her to yourself. She's a peach.'

'You said Estelle Radnor's daughter.'

'Didn't she tell you who she was?'

'No,' Lysandros said, tight-lipped. 'She didn't.'

He moved away in Petra's direction, appalled at the trap into which he'd fallen so easily. His comments about her mother had left him at a disadvantage, something not to be tolerated. She could have warned him and she hadn't, which meant she was laughing at him.

And most men would have been beguiled by her merriment, her way of looking askance, as though that was how she saw the whole world, slightly lopsided, and all the more fun for that.

Fun. He barely knew the word, but something told him she knew it, loved it, even judged by it. And she was doubtless judging him now. His face hardened.

It was too late to catch her; she'd reached the top table where the bride and groom would sit. Now there would be no chance for a while.

A steward showed him to his place, also at the top table but just around the corner at right angles to her—close enough to see her perfectly, but not talk.

She was absorbed in chatting to her companion. Suddenly she laughed, throwing back her head and letting her amusement soar up into the blue sky. It was as though sunshine had burst out all over the world. Unwillingly he conceded that she would be enchanting, if—*if* he'd been in a mood to be enchanted. Fortunately, he was more in control than that.

Then she looked up and caught his eye. Clearly she knew that her little trick had been rumbled, for her teasing gaze said, *Fooled you!*

He sent back a silent message of his own. *Wait, that's all. Just wait!*

She looked forward to it. Her smile told him that, causing a stirring deep within him that he had to conceal by fiercely blanking his face. People sitting close by drew back a little, wondering who had offended him.

There was a distant cheer and applause broke out as Mr and Mrs Homer Lukas made their grand entrance.

He was in his sixties, grey-haired and heavily built with an air of natural command. But as he and his bride swept into place it suited him to bend his head over her hand, kissing it devotedly. She seemed about to faint with joy at his tribute, or perhaps at the five million dollar diamond on her finger.

The young woman who'd dared to tease Lysandros joined in the applause, and kissed her mother as Estelle sat down. The crowd settled to the meal.

Of course he should never have mistaken her for an employee. Her air of being at home in this company ought to have warned him. And when she moved in to take close-up photographs both bride and groom posed at her command.

Then she posed with the happy couple while a professional photographer took the shots. At this point Nikator butted in.

'We must have some of us together,' Lysandros could just hear him cry. 'Brother and sister.'

Having claimed a brother's privilege, he snaked an arm about her waist and drew her close. She played up, but Lysandros spotted a fleeting look of exasperation on her face, and she freed herself as soon as possible, handing him back to Debra Farley like a nurse ridding herself of a pesky child.

Not that he could blame Nikator for his preference. In that glamorous company this creature stood out, with her effortless simplicity and an air of naturalness that the others had lost long ago. Her dress was light blue silk, sleeveless, figure-hugging, without ornament. It was practically a proclamation, as though she were saying, *I need no decoration. I, myself, am enough.*

No doubt about that.

As the party began to break up he made his way over to her. She was waiting for him with an air of teasing expectancy.

'I suppose that'll teach me to be more careful next time,' he said wryly.

'You were a little incautious, weren't you?'

'You thought it was a big joke not to tell me who you were while I said those things about your mother.'

'I didn't force you to say them. What's the matter with you? Can't you take a joke?'

'No,' he said flatly. 'I don't find it funny at all.'

She frowned a little, as though confronting an alien species. 'Do you find anything funny—ever?'

'No. It's safer that way.'

Her humour vanished. 'You poor soul.'

She sounded as though she meant it, and the hint of sympathy took him aback. It was so long since anyone had dared to pity him, or at least dared to show it. Not since another time—another world—long ago...

An incredible suspicion briefly troubled his mind. He ordered it gone and it obeyed, but reluctantly.

'If you feel I insulted your mother, I apologise,' he said stiffly.

'Actually, it's me you insulted.'

'I don't see how.'

She looked into his face with a mixture of incredulity, indignation, but mostly amusement.

'You really don't, do you?' she asked. 'All this time and you still haven't—you *really* haven't—? Well, let me tell you, when you meet a lady for the second time, it's considered polite to remember the first time.'

'For the second—? Have we ever—have we—?'

And then the suspicion wouldn't be banished any longer. He *knew*.

'It was you,' he said slowly. 'On the roof—in Las Vegas—'

'Boy, I really lived in your memory, didn't I?'

'But—you're different—not the same person.'

'I should hope not, after all this time. I'm the same in some ways, not others. You're different too, but you're easier to spot.

I was longing for you to recognise me, but you didn't.' She sighed theatrically. 'Hey ho! What a disappointment!'

'You didn't care if I recognised you or not,' he said flatly.

'Well, maybe just a little.'

An orchestra was getting into place and the dancing area was being cleared, so that they had to move to the side.

He was possessed by a strange feeling, of having wandered into an alien world where nothing was quite as it looked. She had sprung out of the past, landing in his path, challenging him with memories and fears.

'Even now I can't believe that it's you,' he said. 'Your hair's different—it was cut very short—'

'Functional,' she said at once. 'I was surrounded by film people making the best of themselves, so I made the least of myself as an act of adolescent defiance.'

'Was that all you could think of?'

'Consider my problem,' she said with an expansive gesture. 'The average teenager goes wild, indulges herself with wine, late nights, lovers—but everyone around me was doing that. I'd never have been noticed. So I cut my hair as badly as possible, bought cheap clothes, studied my school books and had early nights. Heavens, was I virtuous! Boring but virtuous.'

'And what happened?' he asked, fascinated.

She chuckled. 'My mother started to get very worried about my "strange behaviour". It took her a while to accept the fact that I was heading for the academic life.'

'Doing what?'

'I've made my career out of ancient Greece. I write books, I give lectures. I pretend to know a lot more than I actually do—'

'Like most of them,' he couldn't resist saying.

'Like most of them,' she agreed at once.

'Is your mother reconciled?'

'Oh, yes, she's terribly impressed now. She came to one of my lectures and afterwards she said, "Darling that was wonderful! *I didn't understand a word.*" That's her yardstick, bless her. And in the end it was me who introduced her to Homer.' She looked around. 'So you could say I'm to blame for all this.'

It was time for the dancing. Homer and Estelle took the floor, gliding about in each other's arms until the photographers had all had their fill.

'Aren't you taking any pictures?' he asked.

'No, mine's just the personal family stuff. What they're doing now is for the public.'

Nikator waved as he danced past with Debra in his arms. Petra sighed.

'He may be in his late thirties but he's just a silly kid at heart. What it'll be like when he takes over the firm I can't—' She broke off guiltily, her hand over her mouth. 'I didn't say that.'

'Don't worry. You didn't say anything the whole world doesn't already know. It's interesting that you're learning already.'

There was a sardonic edge to his voice, and she didn't have to ask what he meant. The two great families of Greek shipbuilding survived by getting the edge on each other, and inevitably that included spying. The kind of casual comment that others could risk might be dangerous.

The dance ended and another one began. Debra vanished in the arms of a powerful producer, and Nikator made his way in Petra's direction.

'Oh, heavens, dance with me!' she breathed, seizing Lysandros and drawing him onto the floor.

'What are you—?' Somehow he found his arms around her.

'Yes, I know, in polite society I'm supposed to wait for you to ask me,' she muttered, 'but this isn't polite society, it's a goldfish bowl.'

He felt she couldn't have put it better.

'But your fears may be misplaced,' he pointed out. 'With you being so boring and virtuous he probably wasn't going to ask you at all.'

'He has peculiar tastes.' She added hurriedly, 'And I didn't say that, either.'

She was like quicksilver in his arms, twisting and turning against him, leading him on so that he moved in perfect time with her and had to fight an impulse to tighten his grip, draw her against his body and let things happen as they would. Not here. Not now. Not yet.

Petra read him fairly accurately, and something thrilled in her blood.

'Don't you like dancing?' she asked after a while.

'This isn't dancing. It's swimming around that goldfish bowl.'

'True. But we annoyed Nikator, which is something gained.'

She was right. Nikator's expression was that of a child whose toys had been snatched away. Then Lysandros forgot everything except Petra. Her face was close to his and the smile in her eyes reached him directly.

'What will you do after this?' he asked.

'Stay here for a few days, or weeks. It's a chance for me to do some research. Homer has great contacts. There's a museum vault that's never opened for anyone, but he's fixing it for me.'

He glanced down at the slender, sensual body moving in his arms, at the charming face that seemed to smile more naturally than any other expression, and the blue eyes with their mysterious, tantalising depths, and he knew a sense of outrage. What was this woman doing in museums, investigating the dead, when everything in her spoke of life? She belonged not in tombs but in sunlight, not turning dusty pages but caressing a man's face and pressing her naked body against his.

The mere thought of her nakedness made him draw a sharp breath. The dress fitted her closely enough to give him a good idea of her contours, but it only tempted him to want more. He controlled his thoughts by force.

'Is visiting museums really your idea of being lucky?' he asked slowly.

'I'm going to see things that other scholars have been struggling to see for years. I'll be ahead of the game.'

'But isn't there anything else you want to do?' he asked.

'You mean, what's a woman doing worrying her little head about such things? Women are made for pleasure; serious matters should be left to men.'

Since this came dangerously near to his actual thoughts he was left floundering for a moment. He wished she hadn't used the word 'pleasure'. It was a distraction he could do without.

'I didn't mean it like that,' he managed to say at last, 'but when life offers you so many more avenues—'

'Like Nikator? Yes, I could throw myself into his arms, or anything else he wanted me to throw myself into—careful!'

'Sorry,' he said hastily, loosing his fingers, which he'd tightened against her instinctively.

'Where was I? Ah, yes, exploring avenues.'

'Forget Nikator,' he snapped. 'He's not an avenue, he's a dead end.'

'Yes, I'd managed to work that out for myself. I'm not seventeen any more. I'm thirty-two, in my dotage.'

In her dotage, he thought ironically, with skin like soft peach, hair like silk and eyes that teased, inviting him just so far and warning him against going any further. But she was right about one thing. She was no child. She'd been around long enough to discover a good deal about men, and he had an uneasy feeling that she could read more about him than he wanted her—or anyone—to know.

'If you're fishing for compliments you picked the wrong man,' he said.

'Oh, sure, I'd never come to you for sweet nothings, or for anything except—yes, that would be something—' She hesitated, as though trying to phrase it carefully. 'Something you could give me better than any other man,' she whispered at last.

He struggled not to say the words, but they came out anyway. 'And what's that?'

'Good financial advice,' she declared. 'Aha! There, I did it.'

'Did what?'

'I made you laugh.'

'I'm not laughing,' he said through twitching lips.

'You would be if you weren't trying so hard not to. I bet myself I could make you laugh. Be nice. Give me my little victory.'

'I'm never nice. But I'll let you have it this once.'

'Only this once?' she asked, raising her eyebrows.

'I prefer to claim victory for myself.'

'I could take that as a challenge.'

Then there was silence as their bodies moved in perfect time, and she thought that yes, he was a challenge, and what a challenge he would be; so different from the easy-going men with whom she'd mostly spent her life. There was a darkness about him that he made little attempt to hide, and which tempted her, although she knew she was probably crazy.

'Do your challenges usually work out as you plan?' he asked.

'Oh, yes,' she assured him. 'I won't settle for anything less than my own way.'

'I'm exactly the same. What a terrible battle looms ahead.'

'True,' she said. 'I'm trembling in fear of you.'

He didn't speak, but a slow smile overtook his face—the smile of a man who didn't believe her and was planning a clever move.

Petra had a strange feeling that the other women on the dance floor were staring at her. Most of them had slept with Lysandros, she'd been warned, and suddenly she knew it was true. Their eyes were feverish, full of memories, hot, sweet and glorious, followed by anguish. Mentally they raked her, undressed her, trying to imagine whether she would please him.

And that was really unnerving because she was trying to decide the same thing.

They spoke to her, those nameless women, telling her that he was a lover of phenomenal energy, who could last all night, untiring, driving her on to heights she'd never reached before, heights she wanted to discover.

There was one woman in particular whose greedy gaze caught her attention. Something about the extravagantly dressed, petulant creature made Petra wonder if this was the most recent of Lysandros's conquests—and his rejections. Her eyes were like the others, but a thousand times more bitter, more murderous.

Then Lysandros turned her in the dance, faster and faster, taking her to a distant place where there was only the whirling movement that shut out the rest of the world. She gave herself up to it completely, wanting nothing else.

Would she too lie in his arms in a fever of passion? And would she end up like the others, yearning wretchedly from a distance?

But something told her that their path together wouldn't be as simple as that.

Suddenly they were interrupted by a shout from a few yards off. Everyone stopped dancing and backed away, revealing the bride and groom locked in a passionate embrace. As befitted a glamorous couple, the kiss went on and on as the crowd cheered and applauded. Then some of the others began to embrace. More and more followed suit until it seemed as though the whole place was filled with lingering kisses.

Lysandros stood motionless, his arm still around her waist, the other hand holding hers. The space between them remained barely a centimetre. It would take only the slightest movement for him to cover that last tiny distance and lay his lips on hers. She looked up at him, her heart beating.

'What a performance!' he exclaimed, looking around and speaking in disapproving tones. 'I won't insult you by subjecting you to it.'

He released her, stepping back and giving her no choice but to do the same.

'Thank you,' she said formally. 'It's delightful to meet a man with a sense of propriety.'

She could have hit him.

'I'm afraid I must be going,' he said. 'I've neglected my affairs for too long. It's been a pleasure meeting you again.'

'And you,' she said crisply.

He inclined his head courteously, and in a moment he was gone.

Thunderstruck, she watched him, barely believing what had happened, and so suddenly. He was as deep in desire as herself. All her instincts told her that beyond a shadow of doubt. Yet he'd denied that desire, fought it, overcome it, *because that was what he had decided to do.*

This was a man of steely will, which he would impose no matter what the cost to himself or anyone else. He'd left her without even a glance back. It was like a blow in the stomach.

'Don't worry. Just be patient.'

Petra looked up to see the woman who'd caught her attention while they'd danced. Now she recalled seeing her arrive at the wedding with one of the city's most wealthy and powerful men. She was regarding Petra with a mixture of contempt and pity.

'I couldn't help watching you—and Lysandros,' she said,

moving nearer. 'It's his way, you see. He'll come just so close, and then withdraw to consider the matter. When he's decided that he can fit you in with his other commitments he'll return and take his pleasure at his own time and his own convenience.'

'If I agree,' Petra managed to say.

The woman gave a cold, tinkly laugh.

'Don't be absurd, of course you'll agree. It's written all over you. He could walk back right this minute and you'd agree.'

'I guess you know what you're talking about,' Petra said softly.

'Oh, yes, I know. I've been there. I know what's going through your head because it went through mine. "Who does he think he is to imagine he can just walk back and I'll yield to him on command?" But then he looks at you as if you're the only woman in the world, and you do yield on his command. And it'll be wonderful—for a while. In his arms, in his bed, you'll discover a universe you never knew existed.

'But one day you'll wake up and find yourself back on earth. It will be cold because he's gone. He's done with you. You no longer exist. You'll weep and refuse to believe it, but he won't answer the phone, so after a while you'll have to believe it.'

She began to turn away, but paused long enough to say over her shoulder, 'You think you'll be different, but with him no woman is ever different. Goodbye.'

CHAPTER THREE

THE party went on into the evening. Lights came on throughout the false Parthenon, music wafted up into the sky, assignations were made, profitable deals were settled. Petra accompanied Estelle into the house to help her change into her travelling clothes.

The honeymoon was to be spent on board the *Silver Lady*, Homer's yacht, refurbished for the occasion and currently moored in the port of Piraeus, about five miles away. Two cars bearing luggage and personal servants had already gone on ahead. There remained only the limousine to convey the bride and groom.

'Are you all right?' Estelle asked, glancing at her daughter's face.

'Of course,' Petra said brightly.

'You look as if you were brooding about something.'

In fact she'd been brooding about the stranger's words.

'When he's decided that he can fit you in with his other commitments he'll return and take his pleasure at his own time and his own convenience.'

That was not going to happen, she resolved. If he returned tonight he would find her missing.

'Do you mind if I come to the port to see you off?' she asked suddenly.

'Darling, that would be lovely. But I thought you'd be planning a wild night out.'

'Not me. I don't have your energy.'

In the car on the way to the port they drank champagne. Once on board, Homer showed her around the stately edifice with vast pride, finishing in the great bedroom with the bed big enough for six, covered with gold satin embroidered cushions.

'Now we must find a husband for you,' he declared expansively.

'No, thank you,' Petra hurried to say. 'My one experience of marriage didn't leave me with any desire to try again.'

Before he could reply, her cellphone rang and she answered.

'I'm afraid my manners left something to be desired,' said a man's voice. 'Perhaps I can make amends by taking you to dinner?'

For a moment she floundered. She had her speech of rejection ready prepared but no words would come.

'I'm not sure—'

'My car's just outside the house.'

'But I'm not there. I'm in Piraeus.'

'It won't take you long to return. I'll be waiting.'

He hung up.

'Cheek!' she exploded. 'He just takes it for granted I'll do what he wants.' Seeing them frowning, she added, 'Lysandros Demetriou. He wants to take me to dinner, and I wasn't given much chance to say no.'

'That sounds like him,' Homer said approvingly. 'When he wants something he doesn't waste time.'

'But it's no way to treat a lady,' Estelle said indignantly.

He grinned and kissed her. 'You didn't seem to mind.'

As they were escorting her off the yacht Petra suddenly had a thought.

'How did he know my cellphone number? I didn't give it to him.'

'He probably paid someone in my household to find out,' Homer said as though it was a matter of course. 'Goodbye, my dear.'

She hurried down the gangplank and into the car. On the journey back to Athens she tried to sort out her thoughts. She was angry, but mostly with herself. So many good resolutions ground to dust because of a certain tone in his voice.

On impulse she took out her phone and dialled the number of Karpos, an Athens contact, an ex-journalist whom she knew to be reliable. When he heard what she wanted he drew a sharp breath.

'Everyone's afraid of him,' he said, speaking quickly. 'In fact they're so afraid that they won't even admit their fear, in case he gets to hear and complains that they've made him look bad.'

'That's paranoid.'

'Sure, but it's the effect he has. Nobody is allowed to see inside his head or his heart—if he has one. Opinion is divided about that.'

'But wasn't there someone, a long time ago—? From the other family?'

'Right. Her name was Brigitta, but I didn't tell you that. She died in circumstances nobody has ever been able to discover. The press were warned off by threats, which is why you'll never see it mentioned now.'

'You mean threats of legal action?'

'There are all kinds of threats,' Karpos said mysteriously. 'One man started asking questions. The next thing he knew, all his debts were called in. He was on the verge of ruin, but it was explained to him that if he "behaved himself" in future, matters could be put right. Of course he gave the promise, turned over all his notes, and everything was miraculously settled.'

'Did anything bad happen to him afterwards?'

'No, he left journalism and went into business. He's very successful, but if you say the name Demetriou, he leaves the room quickly. Anything you know, you have to pretend not to know, like the little apartment he has in Athens, or Priam House in Corfu.'

'Priam House?' she said, startled. 'I've heard of that. People have been trying to explore the cellar for years— there's something there, but nobody's allowed in. Do you mean it's his?'

'So they say. But don't let on that you know about it. In fact, don't tell him you've spoken to me, please.'

She promised and hung up. Sitting there, silent and thoughtful, she knew she was getting into deep water. But deep water had never scared her.

She also knew that there was another aspect to this, something that couldn't be denied.

After fifteen years, she and Lysandros Demetriou had unfinished business.

He'd said he would be waiting for her and, sure enough, he was there by the gate to Homer's estate. As her car slowed he pulled open the door, took her hand and drew her out.

'I won't be long,' she said. 'I just have to go inside and—'

'No. You're fine as you are. Let's go.'

'I was going to change my dress—'

'You don't need to. You're beautiful. You know that, so why are we arguing?'

There was something about this blunt speech that affected her more than a smooth compliment would ever have done. He had no party manners. He said exactly what he thought, and he thought she was beautiful. She felt a smile grow inside her until it possessed her completely.

'You know what?' she said. 'You're right. Why are we arguing?' She indicated for her chauffeur to go on without her and got into Lysandros's car.

She wondered where he would take her, possibly a sophisticated restaurant, but he surprised her by driving out into the countryside for a few miles and stopping at a small restaurant, where he led her to an outside table. Here they were close to the coast and in the distance she could just make out the sea, shimmering beneath the moon.

'This is lovely,' she said. 'It's so peaceful after all the crowds today.'

'That's how I feel too,' he said. 'Normally I only come here alone.'

The food was simple, traditional Greek cooking, just as she liked it. While he concentrated on the order Petra had the chance to consider him, trying to reconcile his reputation as a ruthless tyrant with the suffering boy she'd met years ago.

That boy had been vulnerable and still able to show it, to the extent of telling a total stranger that a betrayal of trust had broken his heart. Now he was a man who inspired fear, who would deny having a heart, who would probably jeer at the idea of trust.

What had really happened all those years ago? And could it ever be put right for him?

She thought again of dancing with him, the other women with their envious, lustful glances as they relived hours spent in bed with that tall, strong body, yielding ecstatically to skills they'd found in no other man.

'Are you all right?' Lysandros asked suddenly.

'Yes—why do you ask?'

'You drew a sharp breath, as though you were in pain.'

'No, I'm not in pain,' she hurried to say.

Unless, she thought, you included the pain of wanting something you'd be wiser not to want. She pretended to search her bag. When she glanced up she found him regarding her with a look of wonder.

'Fifteen years,' he said. 'So much has happened and we've changed, and yet in another way we're still the same people. I would have known you anywhere.'

She smiled. 'But you didn't recognise me.'

'Only on the surface. Inside, there was a part of me that knew you. I never thought we'd meet again, and yet somehow I was always certain that we would.'

She nodded. 'Me too. If we'd waited another fifteen years—or fifty—I'd still have been sure that we would one day talk again before we died.'

The last words seemed to reach right inside him. To talk again before they died. That was it. He knew that normally his own thoughts would have struck him as fanciful. He was a strong man, practical, impatient of anything that he couldn't pin down. Yet what he said was true. She'd been an unseen presence in his life ever since that night.

He wondered how he could tell her this. She'd inspired him with the will to talk freely, but that wasn't enough. He didn't know how.

The food arrived, feta and tomato slices, simple and delicious.

'Mmm,' she said blissfully.

He ate little, spending most of his time watching her.

'Why were you up there?' he asked at last. 'Why not downstairs, enjoying the wedding?'

'I guess I'm a natural cynic.' She smiled. 'My grandfather used to say that I approached life with an attitude of, *Oh, yeah?* And it's true. I think it was already there that night in Las Vegas, and it's got worse since. Given the madhouse I've always lived in, it could hardly be any other way.'

'How do you feel about the madhouse?'

'I enjoy it, as long as I'm not asked to get too deeply involved in it or take it seriously.'

'You've never wanted to be a film actress yourself?'

'Good grief, no! One raving lunatic in the family is enough.'

'Does your mother know you talk like that?'

'Of course. She actually said it first, and we're agreed. She's a sweetie and I adore her, but she lives on the Planet Zog.'

'How old is she really?'

'As old as she needs to be at any one moment. She was seventeen when she had me. My father didn't want any responsibility, so he just dumped her, and she struggled alone for a while. Believe me, anyone who just sees her as a film star should see the back streets of London where we lived in those years.

'Then my father's parents got in touch to say that he'd just died in a road accident. They hadn't even known we existed until he admitted it on his deathbed. They were Greek, with strong ideas about family, and I was all the family they had left. Luckily, they were nice people and we all got on well. They looked after me while Estelle built her career. My grandfather was a scholar who'd originally come to England to run a course in Greek at university. At first I didn't even go to school because he reckoned he could teach me better, and he was right.'

'So you grew up as the one with common sense?'

'Well, one of us had to have some,' she chuckled.

'How did you manage with all those stepfathers?'

'They were OK. Mostly they were lovelorn and a bit dopey, so I had a hard job keeping a straight face.'

'What about the one in Las Vegas?'

'Let's see, he was the—no, that was the other one—or was he? Oh, never mind. They're all the same, anyway. I think he was an aspiring actor who thought Estelle could help his ambitions. When she finally saw through him she tossed him out. She was in love with someone else by then.'

'You're very cool about it all. Doesn't all this "eternal love" affect you?'

'Eternal love?' She seemed to consider this. 'Would that be eternal love as in he tried to take every penny she had, or as in he haunted the set, throwing a fit whenever she had a love scene, or as in—?'

'All right, I get the picture. Evidently the male sex doesn't impress you.'

'However did you guess?'

'But what about your own experience? There must have been one or two brave enough to defy the rockets you fire at them?'

Her lips twitched. 'Of course. I don't look at them unless they're brave enough to do that.'

'That's the first of your requirements, is it? Courage?'

'Among other things. But even that's overrated. The man I married was a professional sportsman, a skier who could do the most death-defying stuff. The trouble was, it was all he could do, so in the end he was boring too.'

'You're married?' he asked slowly.

'Not any more,' she said in a tone of such devout thankfulness that he was forced to smile.

'What happened? Was it very soon after our meeting?'

'No, I went to college and studied hard. It was the same college where my grandfather had been a professor, and it was wonderful because people couldn't care less that I was a film star's daughter, but they were impressed that I was his granddaughter. I had to do him credit. I studied to improve my knowledge of the Greek language, learned the history, passed exams. We were going to come here and explore together, but then he and my grandmother both died. It's not the same without him. I so much wanted to make him proud of me.'

She hesitated, while a shadow crossed her face, making him lean forward.

'What is it?' he asked gently.

'Oh—nothing.'

'Tell me,' he persisted, still gentle.

'I was just remembering how much I loved them and they loved me. They needed me, because I was all that was left to them after their son died. They liked Estelle, but she wasn't part of them as I was.'

'Wasn't your mother jealous of your closeness to them?'

Petra shook her head. 'She's a loving mother, in her way, but I've never been vital to her as I was to them.'

'How sad,' he said slowly.

'Not really. As long as you have someone who needs you, you can cope with the others who don't.'

At that moment all the others who hadn't needed her seemed to be there in the shadows, starting with Estelle, always surrounded by people whose job it was to minister to her—hairdressers, make-up artists, lawyers, psychologists, professional comfort-givers, lovers, husbands. Whatever she wanted, there was always someone paid to provide it.

She was sweet-tempered and had showered her daughter with a genuine, if slightly theatrical affection, but when a heavy cold had forced Petra to miss one of her weddings—Fourth? Fifth?—she'd shrugged, said, "Never mind" and merely saved her an extra large piece of cake.

Petra had soon understood. She was loved, but she wasn't essential. She'd tried to take it lightly, saying that it didn't matter, because she'd found that this was one way to cope. Eventually it had become the way she coped with the whole of life.

But it had mattered. There, always at the back of her mind, had been the little sadness, part of her on the lookout for someone to whom she was vitally necessary. Her. Not the money and glamour with which her mother's life surrounded her, but *her*.

And perhaps that was why a young man's agony and desperation had pierced her heart on a roof in Las Vegas fifteen years ago.

'But your grandparents died,' Lysandros said. 'Who do you have now?'

She pulled herself together. 'Are you kidding? My life is crowded with people. It's like living with a flock of geese.'

'Including your mother's husbands?'

'Well, she didn't bother to marry them all. She said there wasn't enough time.'

'Boyfriends?' he asked carefully.

'Some. But half of them were simply trying to get close to my mother, which didn't do my self-confidence any good. I learnt to keep my feelings to myself until I'd sized them up.' She gave a soft chuckle. 'I got a reputation for being frigid.'

They were mad, he thought. No woman who was frigid had that warmth and resonance in her voice, or that glow on her skin.

'And then I met Derek,' she recalled. 'Estelle was making a film with a winter sports background and he was one of the advisors. He was so handsome, I fell for him hook, line and sinker. I thought it had happened at last. We were happy enough for a couple of years, but then—' she shrugged '—I guess he got bored with me.'

'*He* got bored with *you?*' he asked with an involuntary emphasis.

She chuckled as though her husband's betrayal was the funniest thing that had ever happened to her. He was becoming familiar with that defensive note in her laughter. It touched an echo in himself.

'I don't think I was ever the attraction,' she said. 'He needed money and he thought Estelle Radnor's daughter would have plenty. Anyway, he started sleeping around, I lost my temper and I think it scared him a little.'

'You? A temper?'

'Most people think I don't have one because I only lose it once in a blue moon. Now and then I really let fly. I try not to because what's the point? But it's there, and it can make me say things I wish I hadn't. Anyway, that was five years ago. It's all over. Why are you smiling?'

When had anyone last asked him that? When had anyone had cause to? How often did he smile?

'I didn't know I was smiling,' he said hastily.

'You looked like you'd seen some private joke. Come on. Share.'

Private joke! If his board of directors, his bank manager, his underlings heard that they'd think she was delusional.

But the smile was there, growing larger, happier, being drawn forth by her teasing demand.

'Tell me,' she said. 'What did I say that was so funny?'

'It's not—it's just the way you said "It's all over", as though you'd airbrushed the entire male sex out of your life.'

'Or out of the universe,' she agreed. 'Best thing for them.'

'For them, or for you?'

'Definitely for me. Men no longer exist. Now my world is this country, my work, my investigations.'

'But the ancient Greeks had members of the male sex,' he pointed out. 'Unfortunate, but true.'

'Yes, but I can afford to be tolerant about them. They helped start my career. I wrote a book about Greek heroes just before I left university, and actually got it published. Later I was asked to revise it into a less academic version, for schools, and the royalties have been nice. So I feel fairly charitable about the legendary Greek men.'

'Especially since they're safely dead?'

'You're getting the idea.'

'Let's eat,' he said hastily.

The waiter produced chicken and onion pie, washed down with sparkling wine, and for a while there was no more talking. Watching her eat, relishing every mouthful, he wondered about her assertion that men no longer existed for her. With any other woman he would have said it was a front, a pretence to fool the world while she carried on a life of sensual indulgence. But this woman was different. She inhabited her own universe, one he'd never encountered before.

'So that's how you came to know so much that night in Las Vegas,' he said at last. 'You gave me a shock, lecturing me about Achilles.'

She gave a rueful laugh. 'Lecturing. That just about says it all. I'm afraid I do, and people get fed up. I can't blame them. I remember I made you very cross.'

'I wasn't thrilled to be told I was sulking,' he admitted, 'but I was only twenty-three. And besides—'

'And besides, you were very unhappy, weren't you?' she asked. 'Because of *her*.'

He shrugged. 'I don't remember.'

Her gentle eyes said that she didn't believe him.

'She made you trust her, but then you found you couldn't trust her,' she encouraged. 'You don't forget something like that.'

'Would you like some more wine?' he asked politely.

So he wasn't ready to tell her the things she yearned to know, about the catastrophe that had smashed his life. She let it go, knowing that hurrying him would be fatal.

'So your grandfather taught you Greek,' he said, clearly determined to change the subject.

'Inside me, I feel as much Greek as English. He made sure of that.'

'That's how you knew about Achilles? I thought you'd been learning about him at school.'

'Much more than that. I read about him in Homer's *Iliad*, how he was a hero of the Trojan war. I thought that story was so romantic. There was Helen, the most beautiful woman in the world, and all those men fighting over her. She's married to Menelaus but she falls in love with Paris, who takes her to Troy. But Menelaus won't give up and the Greek troops besiege Troy for ten years, trying to get her back.

'And there were all those handsome Greek heroes, especially Achilles,' she went on, giving him a cheeky smile. 'What made your mother admire Achilles rather than any of the others?'

'She came from Corfu where, as you probably know, his influence is very strong. Her own mother used to take her to the Achilleion Palace, although that was chiefly because she was fascinated by Sisi.'

Petra nodded. 'Sisi' had been Elizabeth of Bavaria, a romantic heroine of the nineteenth century, and reputedly the loveliest woman of her day. Her beauty had caused Franz Joseph, the young Emperor of Austria, to fall madly in love with her and sweep her into marriage when she was only sixteen.

But the marriage had faltered. For years she'd roamed the world, isolated, wandering from place to place, until she'd bought a palace on the island of Corfu.

The greatest tragedy of her life was the death of her son Rudolph, at Mayerling, in an apparent suicide pact with his mistress. A year later Sisi had begun to transform the Palace into a tribute to Achilles, but soon she too was dead, at the hands of an assassin. The Palace had subsequently been sold and turned into a museum, dedicated to honouring Achilles.

'The bravest and the most handsome of them all, yet hiding a secret weakness,' Petra mused.

She was referring to the legend of Achilles' mother, who'd sought to protect her baby son by dipping him in the River Styx, that ran between earth and the underworld. Where the waters of the Styx touched they were held to make a man immortal. But she'd held him by the heel, leaving him mortal in the one place where the waters had not touched him. Down the centuries that story resonated so that the term 'Achilles heel' still meant the place where a strong person was unexpectedly vulnerable.

Of all the statues in the Achilleon, the most notable was the one showing him on the ground, vainly trying to pull the arrow from his heel as his life ebbed away.

'In the end it was the thing that killed him,' Lysandros said. 'His weakness wasn't so well-hidden after all. His assassin knew exactly where to aim an arrow, and to cover the tip with poison so that it would be fatal.'

'Nobody is as safe as they believe they are,' she mused.

'My father's motto was—never let anyone know what you're thinking. That's the real weakness.'

'But that's not true,' she said. 'Sometimes you're stronger because other people understand you.'

His voice hardened. 'I disagree. The wise man trusts nobody with his thoughts.'

'Not even me?' she asked softly.

She could tell the question disconcerted him, but his defences were too firmly riveted in place to come down easily.

'If there was one person I could trust—I think it would be you, because of the past. But I am what I am.' He gave a self-mocking smile. 'I don't think even you can change me.'

She regarded him gently before venturing to touch his hand.

'Beware people you think you can trust?' she whispered.

'Did I say that?' he asked quickly.

'Something like it. In Las Vegas, you came to the edge of saying a lot more.'

'I was in a bad way that night. I don't know what I said.'

A silence came down over him. He stared into his glass,

and she guessed that he was shocked at himself for having relented so far. Now he would retreat again behind walls of caution and suspicion.

Was there any way to get through to this man's damaged heart? she wondered. And, if she tried, might she not do him more harm than good?

CHAPTER FOUR

'I'M SORRY,' Lysandros said quietly. 'This is me; it's who and what I am.'

'You don't let anyone in, do you?' Petra said.

He shook his head with an air of finality. Suddenly then he said, 'But I will tell you one thing. It may only be a coincidence, but it's strange. After I'd taken you back to your room I returned to the tables and suddenly started winning back everything I'd lost. I just couldn't lose, and somehow that was connected with you, as though you'd turned me into a winner. Why are you smiling?'

'You, being superstitious. If I'd said all that you'd make some snooty masculine comment about women having overly vivid imaginations.'

'Yes, I probably would,' he admitted. 'But perhaps you just exercise a more powerful brand of magic.'

'Magic?'

'Don't tell me you've studied the Greek legends without discovering magic?'

'Yes,' she conceded, 'you meet it in the most unexpected places, and the hard part is knowing how to tell it from wishful thinking.'

She spoke the last words so softly that he barely heard

them, but they were enough to give him a strange sensation, part pleasure, part pain, part alarm.

'Wishful thinking,' he echoed slowly. 'The most dangerous thing on earth.'

'Or the most valuable,' she countered quickly. 'All the great ideas started life as wishful thinking. Wasn't there an ancestor of yours who thought, *I wish I could build a boat*? So he built one, then another one, and here you are.'

'You're a very clever woman.' He smiled. 'You can turn anything around, just by the light you throw on it. The light doesn't just illuminate; it transforms all the things that might have served as a warning.'

'But perhaps they should be transformed,' she pointed out. 'Some people become suspicious so quickly that they need to come off-guard and enjoy a bit of wishful thinking.'

'I said you were clever. Talking like that, you almost convince me. Just as you convinced me back then. Maybe it really is magic. Perhaps you have a brand of magic denied to all other women.'

There was a noise behind him, reminding him that they were in a public place. Reluctantly he released her hand, assuming a calm demeanour, although with an effort.

A small buzz came from his inner pocket. He drew out his phone and grimaced at the text message he found there.

'Damn! I was planning to go to Piraeus tomorrow in any case, but now I think I'd better go tonight. I'll be away for a few days.'

Petra drew a long breath, keeping her face averted. Until then she'd told herself that she wasn't quite sure how she wanted the evening to end, but now she had to be honest with herself. An evening spent talking, beginning to open their hearts, should have led to a night in each other's arms, expressing their closeness in another way. And only now that it was being denied to her did she face how badly she wanted to make love with him.

'Will you be here when I get back?' he asked.

'Yes, I'm staying for a while.'

'I'll call you.'

'We'd better go,' she agreed. 'You have to be on your way.'

'I'm sorry—'

'Don't be,' she said cheerfully. 'It's been a long day. I was fighting to stay awake.'

She wondered if he would actually believe that.

When they reached the Lukas villa the great gates swung open for them, almost as though someone had been watching for their arrival. At the house he opened the car door and came up the steps with her. She looked up at him, curious about his next move.

'Do you remember that night?' he asked gently. 'You were such an innocent that I made you go to bed and saw you to the door.'

'And told me to lock it,' she recalled.

Neither of them mentioned the other thing he'd done, the kiss so soft that it had been barely a whisper against her lips— a kiss without passion, only gentle concern and tenderness. It had lingered with her long after that evening, through days and weeks, then through years. Since then she had known desire and love, but nothing had ever quite erased the memory of that moment. Looking at him now, she knew why, and when he bent his head she longed for it to be the same.

He didn't disappoint her. His lips lay against hers for the briefest possible time before retreating, almost as though he'd found something there that disconcerted him.

'Goodnight,' he said quietly.

He left her before she could react, going down to the car and driving away without looking back, moving fast, as though making his escape.

'Goodnight,' she whispered.

It was only when he was out of sight that she remembered she hadn't asked him how he'd known her phone number.

Petra soon found that her hours were full. Her reputation had gone before her, ensuring that several societies contacted her, asking her to join their excursions or talk to them. She accepted as many invitations as possible. They filled the hours that passed without a word from Lysandros.

One invitation that particularly attracted her came from The Cave Society, a collection of English enthusiasts who were set on exploring an island in the Aegean Sea, about twenty miles out. It was a mass of caves, some of which were reputed to contain precious historical relics.

Nikator was scathing about the idea, insisting that the legend had been rubbished years ago, but the idea of a day out in a boat attracted her.

'Mind you, the place I'd really like to see is Priam House, on Corfu,' she told him. 'Is it true that Lysandros owns it?'

He shrugged. 'I think so.'

She was mostly free of Nikator's company. He spent much time away from home, leaving her free to explore Homer's magnificent library. Sometimes she would take out a tiny photograph she kept in her bag and set it on the table to watch over her.

'Like you watched over me when you were alive, Grandpa,' she told the man in the picture, speaking in Greek.

He was elderly, with a thin, kindly face and a hesitant smile. When he was alive that smile had always been there for her.

He had told her about her father, which Estelle hadn't been able to do very fully. And he'd shown her pictures, revealing her own facial likeness to the young man whose life had been cut short.

But there had been another likeness.

'He had a hasty temper,' Grandpa had said sadly. 'He didn't

mean to be unkind, but he spoke first and thought afterwards.' He'd looked at her tenderly. 'And you're just the same.'

It was true. She was naturally easy-going, but without warning a flash of temper would come streaking out of the darkness, making her say things she afterwards regretted. She'd fought to overcome it and had succeeded in dampening it down to the point when few people ever detected its existence. But it was still there, ready to undermine her without warning.

In the final months of her marriage it had made her say things that would have made a reconciliation impossible, even if she'd wanted one. Right now it was probably a good thing that Lysandros wasn't there to hear the thoughts that were bouncing around like Furies in her brain, demanding expression.

One evening Nikator returned home suddenly and locked himself in his room, refusing to open to anyone, even Petra.

'Perhaps Debra will come to see him,' she suggested to Aminta, the housekeeper.

'No, she's gone back to America,' Aminta said hurriedly.

'I thought she was here until next week.'

'She had to leave suddenly. I should be getting on with my work.'

She scuttled away.

It might mean anything or nothing, Petra thought, and she would probably never know. But for a while Aminta avoided her.

Nikator finally emerged, with a slight swelling on his lips which he refused to discuss beyond saying he'd had a fall. Petra didn't feel like pursuing the subject, but she made a mental note to spend as much time out of the house as possible.

Since the evening of the wedding she'd seen Lysandros only once and that was by chance at a grand banquet given by the city authorities. He'd made his way over to her and said courteously that he hoped she was enjoying Athens. He'd mentioned contacting her again in the next few days, but made no specific plans.

He seemed to be alone. No lady had been invited to accompany him to this occasion, just as her own invitation had made no mention of a guest. She was left wondering at whose behest she had been invited.

After their evening together she had been in turmoil. Behind Lysandros's civilised veneer she sensed a man who was frighteningly alone, locked in a prison of isolation, seeking a way out, yet reluctant to take it. It didn't matter that their first meeting had been so long ago. It had left them both with the sense that they knew each other, and under its influence he'd begun the first tentative movements of reaching out to her. Yet he'd been able only to go so far, then no further. Try as he might, the prison bars had always slammed shut at the last moment.

Her heart ached for him. The pain he couldn't fight had affected her, and she would have rescued him if she could. But in the end it was his own nature that stood in the way, and she knew she could never get past that unless he allowed her.

At night she would relive the brief kiss that he'd given her. Any other man would have seized her in his arms and kissed her breathless, which, truth to tell, she'd half hoped he would do. Instead, he'd behaved with an almost Victorian propriety, caressing her lips in a way that called back that other time when he'd thought only of protecting her. And in doing so he'd touched her heart more than passion would ever do.

But there was passion, she knew that. She couldn't be so close to him without reading the promise of his tall, hard body, the easy movements, the power held in check, ready to be unleashed. Nor could she misunderstand the look in his eyes when they rested on her, thinking her unaware. Some day—and that day must come soon—she would break his control and tempt him beyond endurance.

But gradually her despondency gave way to annoyance. Now she could hear the strange woman at the wedding again, warning her that she was one of many and would yield as easily as the others.

'No way,' she muttered. 'If you think that, boy, have you got a shock coming!'

Briskly she informed the household that she would be away for few days, and was in her room packing a light bag when her phone rang and Lysandros's voice said, 'I'd like to see you this evening.'

She took a moment to stop herself exploding at his sheer cheek, and managed to say calmly, 'I'm about to leave for a few days.'

'Can it wait until tomorrow?'

'I'm afraid not. I'm really very busy. It's been a pleasure knowing you. Goodbye.' She hung up.

'Good for you,' Nikator said from the doorway. 'It's about time somebody told him.'

'It's kind of you to worry about me, Nikki, but I promise you there's no need. I'm in charge. I always have been. I always will be.'

The phone rang again.

'I know you're angry,' Lysandros said. 'But am I beyond forgiveness?'

'You misunderstand,' she said coolly. 'I'm not angry, merely busy. I'm a professional with work to do.'

'You mean I really am beyond forgiveness?'

'No, I—there's nothing to forgive.'

'I wish you'd tell me that to my face. I've been inconsiderate, but I didn't…that is…help me, Petra—please.'

It was as though he'd thrown a magic switch. His arrogance she could fight, but his plea for help reached out to touch her own need.

'I suppose I could rearrange my plans,' she said slowly.

'I'm waiting by the gate. Come as you are; that's all I ask.'

'I'm on my way.'

'You're mad,' Nikator said. 'You know that, don't you?'

She sighed. 'Yes, I guess so. But it can't be helped.'

She escaped his furious eyes as soon as she could. Now she could think of nothing but that Lysandros wanted her. The thought of seeing him again made her heart leap.

He was where he'd said he would be. He didn't kiss her or make any public show of affection, but his hand held hers tightly for a moment and he whispered, 'Thank you,' in a fervent voice that wiped out the days of frustrated waiting.

Darkness was falling as Lysandros took her into the heart of town, finally stopping at a small restaurant that spilled out onto the pavement. From here they could look up at the floodlit Parthenon, high on the Acropolis, dominating all of Athens.

The waiter appeared, politely enquiring if they were ready to visit the kitchen. Petra was familiar with this habit of allowing customers to see the food being prepared, and happily followed him in. Delicious aromas assailed them at once, and it took time to go around trying to make a choice. At last they settled on fried calamari followed by lamb fricassee and returned to the table.

For a while the food and wine occupied her. Sometimes she glanced up to find him watching her with an intense expression that told her all she wanted to know about the feelings he couldn't put into words. For her it was enough to know that he had those feelings. The words could wait.

At last he said politely, 'Have you been busy?'

'I've been doing a lot of reading in Homer's library. I've had some invitations to go on expeditions.'

'And you've accepted them?'

'Not all. How has your work been?'

'No different from usual. Problems to be overcome. I tried
to keep busy because…because…' his voice changed abruptly
'…when I was alone I thought of you.'

'You hid it very well,' she pointed out.

'You mean I didn't call you. I meant to a thousand times,
but I always drew back. I think you know why.'

'I'm not sure I do.'

'You're not like other women. Not to me. With you it has
to be all or nothing, and I—'

'You're not ready for "all",' she finished for him. Without
warning her temper gave a sudden, disconcerting flare. 'That's
fine, because neither am I. Are you suggesting that I was
chasing you?'

'No, I didn't mean that,' he said hastily. 'I was just trying
to apologise.'

'It's all right,' she said.

In fact it wasn't all right. Her contented mood of a moment
ago had faded. The strain of the last few days was catching
up with her, and she was becoming edgy. She'd wanted him
and he'd as good as snubbed her.

Suddenly the evening was on the verge of collapse.

'Can I have a little more wine?' she asked, holding out her
glass and smiling in a way that should have warned him.

He took the hint and abandoned the apology, making her
feel instantly guilty. He was doing his best, but these were un-
charted seas for him. It was she who held the advantage.
Resolutely, she worked to lighten the atmosphere.

'Actually,' she said between sips, 'the most exciting thing
that's happened to me is an invitation from The Cave Society.'

She told him about the letter. Like Nikator, he was sceptical.

'I'm not swallowing it hook, line and sinker,' she assured
him. 'I'm too much of an old hand for that.'

'*Old* hand,' he murmured, regarding her appreciatively.

'Very old. In terms of my reputation, I'm ancient. This—' she pointed to her luxuriant golden mane '—is just dye to hide the fact that I'm white-haired. Any day now I'm going to start walking with a stick.'

'Will you stop talking nonsense?'

'Why?' she asked, genuinely puzzled. 'Nonsense is fun.'

'Yes, but—' He retired, defeated. It wasn't possible to say that the contrast between her words and the young, glorious reality was making him dizzy.

'Oh, all right,' she conceded, 'I don't think there's anything to be found in those caves. On the other hand, I'll usually go anywhere and do anything for a "find", so perhaps I should.'

'But what are you going to find that thousands of others have failed to find?'

'Of course they failed,' she teased, 'because they weren't me. Something is lying there, waiting for me to appear from the mists of time—knowing that the glory of the discovery belongs to me, and only me. Next thing you know, they'll put my statue up in the Parthenon.'

She caught sight of his face and burst out laughing.

'I'm sorry,' she choked, 'but if you could see your expression!'

'You were joking, weren't you?' he asked cautiously.

'Yes, I was joking.'

'I'm afraid I'm a bit—' He shrugged. 'It can be hard to tell.'

'Oh, you poor thing,' she said. 'I know you can laugh. I actually heard you, at the wedding reception, but somehow—'

'It's just—'

'I know,' she said. 'You think too great a sense of humour is a weakness, so you keep yours in protective custody, behind bolts and bars, only to be produced at certain times.'

Lysandros tried to speak, to make some light-hearted remark that would pass the matter off, but inwardly he felt himself retreating from her. Her words, though kindly meant, had been like a lamp shone into his soul, revealing secrets. Not to be tolerated.

'Are you ready for the next course?' he asked politely.

'Yes, please.'

It was definitely a snub, yet she was swept by tenderness and pity for him. He was like a man walking a path strewn with boulders, not knowing they were there until he fell and hurt himself.

And she had a sad feeling that she was the only person in the world who saw him like this, and therefore the only person able to help him.

If only she could, she thought with a qualm of self-doubt. She was still feeling her way tentatively. Suppose she persuaded him to trust her, then faltered and let him down, abandoning him again to mistrust and desolation? Suddenly that seemed like the greatest crime in the world.

As the waiter served them she became aware that a man and a woman were hovering close, trying to get a look at her. When she looked straight at them, they jumped.

'It *is* her,' the woman breathed. 'It *is* you, isn't it?' Then, pulling herself together, she said, 'You really are Petra Radnor?'

'Yes, I am.'

'I saw you on a talk show on television just before we left England, and I've read your books. Oh, this is *such* a thrill.'

There was nothing to do but be polite. Lysandros invited them to sit at the table. His manner was charming, and she wondered if he secretly welcomed the interruption.

'I'm just learning that Miss Radnor is a celebrity,' he said. 'Tell me about her.'

They plunged in, making Petra groan with embarrassment. They were Angela and George, they belonged to The Cave Society and had only just arrived in Athens.

'Our President told us that he'd written to you,' Angela bubbled. 'You will accept our invitation to come to the island, won't you? It would mean so much to us to have a real figure of authority.'

'Please,' Petra said hastily, 'I am not a figure of authority.'

'Oh, but you—'

It went on and on. Petra began to feel trapped. Vaguely she was aware that Lysandros's phone had rung. He answered and his face was instantly full of alarm.

'Of course,' he said sharply. 'We'll come at once.' He hung up. 'I'm afraid there's a crisis. That was my secretary to say I must return immediately, also Miss Radnor, whose presence is essential.'

With a gesture he summoned the waiter, paying not only for his meal and hers but whatever their guests had consumed.

'Good evening,' he said, rising to his feet and drawing her with him. 'It's been a pleasure meeting you.'

They made their escape, running until they were three streets away. Then, under the cover of darkness, he pulled her into his arms.

'Now!' he said.

CHAPTER FIVE

PLEASURE and relief went through her. She had wanted this so much, and now everything in her yearned towards him. Her mouth was ready for him but so was every inch of her body. As he grasped her, so she grasped him, caressing him with hands and lips.

'How did you arrange for the phone to ring?' she gasped.

'It didn't. I simply pressed a button that set the bell off, then I pretended to answer. I had to get you away from there, get you to myself.'

He kissed her again, and his kiss was everything she'd wanted since their meeting. Nothing else in her life had been like it. Nothing else ever would be. It was the kiss she'd secretly longed for since he'd cheated her with a half-kiss all those years ago.

'What have you done to me?' he growled. 'Why can't I stop you doing it?'

'You could if you really wanted to,' she whispered against his mouth. 'Why don't you…why don't you…?'

'Stop tormenting me—'

At that she laughed. Why should she make it easy for him?

'Siren—witch—'

But his lips caressed her even as they hurled names at her.

He was in the grip of a power stronger than himself, and that was just how she wanted him.

From far in the distance an unwelcome sound broke into her joy. It came closer and she realised that a crowd of youngsters had appeared at the end of the street, singing, dancing, chanting up into the sky. Then she recalled that this was European Music Night, when Athens was filled with public celebration.

The crowd passed them, offering good wishes to a couple so profitably engaged. Lysandros grasped her hand and began to run again, but there was no escape. Another crowd appeared from another side street, and another. Seeking an exit, they found themselves in an open square where a rock band was playing on a makeshift stage.

'Where can you get privacy in this place?' Lysandros roared.

'You can't,' Petra cried. She was laughing now, every nerve in her body thrumming with joy. 'There's no privacy; there's only music and laughter—and whatever else you want—'

'It's not funny,' he growled.

'But it is, it is—can't you see—? Oh, darling, please try to understand—please try—'

He relented and touched her face. 'Whatever you say.'

He wasn't quite sure what he meant by that, but he knew they'd come to a place where she was at home, sure-footed, able to lead without faltering. A wise man would accept that and, since he prided himself on his wisdom, he did the sensible thing and let her lead him into the dance.

All about them the other couples swung around, while the band hollered. He knew nothing except that he was looking down at her face and she was laughing, not with amusement but with joy and triumph, inviting him to share. Once, long ago, she'd taken his hand and led him through the tunnel to success. Now she could do it again, except that this success would be different, not a matter of money and crushing foes, but a joyous richness and light, streaming ahead, leading to new life, and whatever that life might bring.

'Let's go,' he cried.

'Where?' she called back in delight.

'Anywhere—wherever you want to take me.'

'Then come.'

She began to run, taking him with her, not knowing where she was heading or why; only knowing that she was with him and that was enough. Now the whole of Athens seemed to be flaming around them.

She stopped at last and they stood, gasping together, their chests heaving. From overhead came the sound of fireworks racing up into the black sky, exploding in an orgy of light, while down below the crowd cried out its pleasure.

'Phew!' she said.

He gave a sigh of agreement and she thumped him lightly.

'You shouldn't be out of breath. I thought you worked out every morning in the gym.'

He did exactly that, and was fully as fit as she expected, but in her company his breathlessness had another cause. He reached for her. Petra saw the firework colours flash across his face, and then his arms were tight about her and his mouth was on hers, teasing, provoking, demanding, imploring.

'Who are you?' he gasped. 'What are you doing in my life? Why can't I—?'

'Hush, it doesn't matter. Nothing matters but this. Kiss me—kiss me.'

She proceeded to show him what she meant, sensing the response go through him, delighting in her power over him and his over her. Soon they must reach the moment that had been inevitable since their meeting, and everything in her yearned towards it.

Lysandros felt as if he were awaking from a dream, or sinking into one. He wasn't sure which. Her plea of 'Kiss me' was entrancing, yet something deep inside him was drawing away. He tried to fight it. He wanted her, but so much that it alarmed him.

Impulse had made him call her tonight. Impulse had made him drag her away from their unwanted companions. Impulse—the thing he'd battled for years—was beginning to rule him.

A puppet dancing on the end of her chain. And she knew it.

'What is it?' she asked, feeling him draw away.

'This place is very public. We should get back to the table; I think I left something there.'

'And then?' she asked slowly, unwilling to believe the thought that was coming into her head.

'Then I think we should both—go home.'

She stared at him, trying to believe what he was doing, feeling the anger rise within her. He hadn't left anything behind and they both knew it. But he was telling her the magic was over. He'd banished it by an act of will, proving that his control was still strong, although he'd brought her to the edge of losing hers.

It was a demonstration of power, and she was going to make him regret it.

'How dare you?' she said in a soft, furious voice. 'Who the hell do you think you are to despise me?'

'I don't—'

'Shut up. I have something to say and you're going to listen. I am not some desperate female who you can pick up and put down when it suits you. And don't pretend you don't know what I mean because you know exactly. They're all standing in line for you, aren't they? But not me.'

'I don't know who gave you such an idea,' he grated.

'Any woman you've ever known could have given it to me. Your reputation went before you.'

His own anger rose.

'I'll bet Nikator had something to say, but are you mad enough to listen to him? Don't tell me he fools you with that "little brother" act!'

'Why shouldn't I believe he's concerned about me?' she demanded.

'Oh, he's concerned all right, but not as a brother. The rumours about him are very interesting at the moment. Why do you think Debra Farley left Athens so suddenly? Because he went too far, wouldn't take no for an answer. Have a look at his face and see what she did to it when she was fighting him off. I gather it took a lot of money to get her to leave quietly.'

'I don't believe it,' she said, ignoring the whispers within her brain.

'I do not tell lies,' Lysandros snapped.

'No, but you can get things wrong. Even the great, infallible Lysandros Demetriou makes mistakes, and you've really made one about me. One minute you say you'll follow "anywhere I want to take you". The next moment it's time to go home. Do you really think I'll tamely accept that sort of behaviour?

'What am I supposed to do now, Lysandros? Sit by the phone, hoping you'll get in touch, like one of those Athens wives? When you called tonight I should have told you to go and jump in the lake—'

'But you didn't, so perhaps we—'

The words were like petrol on flames.

'Well, I'm doing it now,' she seethed. 'You have your work to do, I have mine, and there's no need for us to trouble each other further. Goodnight.'

Turning swiftly away before he could reach out, she hurried back through the streets to the little restaurant. George and Angela were still there, beaming at the sight of Petra.

'We just knew you'd come back,' Angela said. 'You will come to the cave, won't you?'

'Thank you, I look forward to it,' Petra said firmly. 'Why don't we discuss the details now?' She smiled at Lysandros with deadly intent. 'I'll get a taxi home. Don't let us keep you. I'm sure you're busy.'

'You're right,' he said in a forced voice. 'Goodnight. It's been a pleasure meeting you all.'

He inclined his head to them all and was gone. Nor did he look back, which Petra thought was just as well, or he would have seen a look of misery on her face that she wouldn't have admitted for all the world.

Lysandros awoke in a black depression. Now the magical sunshine that had flooded the path ahead had died, replaced by the prosaic everyday light of the city. She wasn't here, and it shamed him to remember how her presence had made him act.

'Wherever you want to take me.' Had he really said that?

He should be glad that she'd hurled the reminder at him, warning him of the danger into which he'd been sleepwalking, saving him in time.

In time?

He rose and went through the process of preparing for the day, moving like an automaton while his brain seethed.

She alarmed him. She mattered too much. Simply by being herself she could lure him out of the armoured cave where he lived, and where he had vowed to stay for the rest of his days.

For years women had come and gone in his life. He'd treated them well in a distant fashion, and seen them depart without regret. But this woman had broken the mould, and he knew that he must cut ties now or risk yielding to weakness, the thing he dreaded most in the world.

He went to his desk, meaning to write a polite letter, accepting her dismissal. That way he wouldn't have to hear her voice with its soft resonance, its memory of pleasure half experienced, still anticipated. He drew paper towards him and prepared to write.

But the pen seemed to have developed a life of its own, and refused to do his bidding. His brain shut down, denying him the necessary words.

This was her doing. She was like one of the sirens of legend, whose voices had lured sailors onto the rocks. How much had they known, those doomed men? Had they gone unknowingly to their death, or had they recognised the truth about the siren-song, yet still been drawn in, unable to help themselves? And when it had been too late, and they sank beneath the waves, had they cursed themselves for yielding, or had their suffering been worth it for the glimpse of heaven?

He would have given anything to know.

At last he gave up trying to write. It was she who had broken it off, and there was nothing more to be said. More business problems made another journey to the port essential, and for several days he had no time to think of anything else. On the journey back to Athens he was able to relax in the feeling of having regained command of his life.

Petra would have replaced him with another eager suitor, and that was best for both of them. He was even glad of it. So he told himself.

On the last mile home he switched on his car radio to hear the latest news. A commentator was describing a search taking place at sea, where a boat had been found overturned. Those aboard had been exploring a cave on an island in the gulf.

'One of those missing is known to be Petra Radnor, daughter of film star Estelle Radnor, who recently married—'

He pulled over sharply to the side of the road and sat in frozen stillness, listening.

She'd said she'd go anywhere and do anything for a 'find', but had she really wanted to go? Hadn't she tried to slide out of it, but then fallen back into the clutches of George and Angela only because of him?

If she hadn't been angry with me she wouldn't have gone on this trip. If she's dead, it's my doing—like last time— like last time—

At last life came back to his limbs. He swung the car round in the direction of the coast, driving as though all the devils in hell were after him.

Night was falling as he reached the sea and headed for the place where the boats were to be found. Outwardly he was calm but he couldn't stop the words thrumming in his head.

She's dead—she's dead—you had your chance and it's gone—again—

A crowd had gathered in the harbour, gazing out to the water and a boat that was heading towards them. Lysandros parked as close as he could and ran to where he could have a better view of the boat.

'They've rescued most of them,' said a man nearby. 'But I heard there was still someone they couldn't find.'

'Does anyone know who?' Lysandros asked sharply.

'Only that it was a woman. I doubt if they'll find her now.'

You killed her—you killed her!

He pressed against the rail, straining his eyes to see the boat coming through the darkness. In the bow stood a woman, huddled in a blanket, as though she'd been rescued from the water. Frantically he strained to see more, but her face was a blur. A passing light suggested that her hair might be light. It could be Petra—if only he could be sure.

His heart was thundering and he gripped the railing so

hard that his hands hurt. It must be her. She couldn't be dead, because if she were—

Shudders racked him.

Suddenly a shout went up, followed by a cheer. The boat was closer now and at last he could see the woman. It was Petra.

He stood there, holding the rail for support, taking deep breaths, trying to bring himself under control.

She would be here in a few moments. He must plan, be organised. A cellphone. That was it! She would have lost hers in the water, but she'd need one to call her mother. He could do that to please her.

Her eyes were searching the harbour until at last she began to wave. Full of joyful relief, Lysandros waved back, but then realised that she wasn't looking at him but at someone closer. Then he saw Nikator dart forward, reaching up to her. She leaned down, smiling and calling to him.

Lysandros stayed deadly still as the boat docked and the passengers streamed off seeking safety. Petra went straight into Nikator's arms and they hugged each other. Then Nikator took out his cellphone, handing it to her, saying things Lysandros couldn't hear, but could guess. Petra dialled, put the phone to her ear and cried, 'Estelle, darling, it's me, I'm safe.'

He didn't hear the rest. He backed hastily into the darkness before hurrying to find his car. Then he departed as quickly as he could.

She never saw him.

Aminta took charge of her as soon as she reached home, making her have a hot bath, eat well and go to bed.

'It was all over the news,' she told Petra. 'We were so worried. Whatever happened?'

'I don't really know. At first it just seemed like an ordinary storm, but suddenly the waves got higher and higher and we overturned. Did you say it was on the news?'

'Oh, yes, about how you were all drowning and they couldn't rescue everyone.'

'There's one woman they're still looking for,' Petra sighed.

She slept badly and awoke in a dark mood. Somewhere in the house she heard the phone ring, and a moment later Aminta brought it in to her.

'It's for you,' she said. 'A man.'

Eagerly she waited to hear Lysandros's voice, full of happiness that she was safe. But it was George, to tell her that the missing woman had been found safe and well. She talked politely for a while, but hung up with relief.

There was no call from Lysandros. The news programmes must have alerted him to her danger, yet the man who had kissed her with such fierce intensity had shown no interest in her fate.

She couldn't blame him after the way she'd ordered him out of her life, yet the hope had persisted that he cared enough to check that she was safe. Apparently not.

She'd been fooling herself. Such interest as he'd ever had in her had been superficial and was now over. He couldn't have said so more clearly.

Nikator was waiting for her when she went downstairs.

'You shouldn't have got up so soon,' he said. 'After what you've been through. Go back to bed and let me look after you.'

She smiled. It had been good to find him on the quay to take her home, and she was feeling friendly towards him. For the next few days he behaved perfectly, showing brotherly kindness without ever crossing the line. It was bliss to relax in his care. Now she was sure that the stories about him weren't true.

If only Lysandros would call her.

* * *

After several days with no sign from Petra, Lysandros called her cellphone, without success. It was still functioning, but it had been switched off. It remained off all the rest of that day, through the night and into the morning.

It made no sense. She could have switched to the answer service; instead, she'd blocked calls completely.

He refused to admit to a twinge of alarm. But at last he yielded and called the Lukas house, getting himself put through to Homer's secretary.

'I need to speak to Miss Radnor,' he said gruffly. 'Be so kind as to ask her to call me.'

'I'm sorry, sir, but Miss Radnor is no longer here. She and Mr Nikator left for England two days ago.'

Silence. When he could manage to speak normally, he said, 'Did she leave any address or contact number?'

'No, sir. She and Mr Nikator said that they didn't want to be disturbed by anyone, for a long time.'

'What happens in an emergency?'

'Mr Nikator said no emergency could matter beside—'

'I see. Thank you.' He hung up abruptly.

At the Lukas mansion the secretary looked around to where Nikator stood in the doorway.

'Did I do all right?' she asked.

'Perfect,' he told her. 'Just keep telling that story if there are any more calls.'

Lysandros sat motionless, his face hard and set.

She's gone—she's not coming back—

The words called to him out of the past, making him shudder.

She's gone—

It meant nothing. She had every right to leave. It was different from the other time.

You'll never see her again—never again—never again—

His fist slammed into the wall with such force that a picture fell to the ground and smashed. A door opened behind him.

'Get out,' he said without looking around.

The door closed hastily. He continued to sit there, staring— staring into the darkness, into the past.

At last he rose like a man in a dream and went up to his room, where he threw a few clothes into a bag. To his secretary he said, 'I'll be away for a few days. Call me on the cell-phone if it's urgent. Otherwise, deal with it yourself.'

'Can I tell anyone where you are?'

'*No.*'

He headed for the airport and caught the next flight to the island of Corfu. To have used his private jet would have been to tell the world where he was going, and that was the last thing he wanted.

In Corfu he owned Priam House, a villa that had once belonged to his mother. It was his refuge, the place he came to be alone, even to the extent of having no servants. There he would find peace and isolation, the things he needed to save him from going mad.

The only disturbance might come from students and ar-chaeologists, attracted by the villa's history. It had been built on the ruins of an ancient temple, and rumours abounded of valuable relics that might still be found.

Light was fading as the villa came into sight, silent and shuttered. He left the taxi while there was still a hundred yards to go, so that he might approach unnoticed.

He opened the gate noiselessly and walked around the side of the villa. All seemed quiet and relief flooded him. At last he let himself in at the back and went through the hall to the stairs. But before he could climb he saw something that made him freeze.

The door to the cellar was standing open.

It was no accident. The cellar led directly to the foundations and that door was always kept locked for reasons of safety. Only he had the key.

Rage swept through him at having his solitude destroyed. At that moment he could have done violence. But his fury was cold, enabling him to go down the stairs and approach his quarry noiselessly.

Someone was in the far corner of the cellar with only one small light that they were using to examine the stones, so that the person couldn't be seen.

'Stop right there,' he said harshly. 'You don't understand the danger you're in. I won't tolerate this. I allow nobody in here.'

He heard a gasp as the intruder made a sharp movement. The torch fell to the floor. His hand shot out in the darkness, found a body, seized it, grappled with it, brought it down.

'Now,' he gasped, 'you're going to be sorry you did this. Let's look at you.'

He reached over for the torch that lay on the flagstones and shone it directly into his enemy's face. Then he froze with shock.

'Petra!'

CHAPTER SIX

PETRA lay looking up at him, her eyes wide, her breath coming in short gasps. Hurriedly he got to his feet, drawing her up with him and holding her, for she was shaking.

'You,' he said, appalled. '*You!*'

'Yes, I'm afraid so.'

She swayed as she spoke and he tightened his grip lest she fall. Swiftly he picked her up and carried her out of the cellar and up the stairs to his room, where he laid her gently on the bed and sat beside her.

'Are you mad to do such a thing?' he demanded hoarsely. 'Have you any idea of the danger you were in?'

'Not real danger,' she said shakily.

'I threw you down onto stone slabs. The floor's uneven; you might have hit your head—I was in such a rage—'

'I'm sorry, I know I shouldn't—'

'The hell with that! You could have died. Do you understand that? *You could have died and then I—*' A violent shudder went through him.

'My dear,' she said gently, 'you're making too much of this. I'm a bit breathless from landing so hard, but nothing more.'

'You don't know that. I'm getting you a doctor—'

'You will not,' she said firmly. 'I don't need a doctor. I haven't broken anything, I'm not in pain and I didn't hit my head.'

He didn't reply but looked at her, haggard. She took his face between her hands. 'Don't look like that. It's all right.'

'It isn't,' he said desperately. 'Sometimes I lose control—and do things without thinking. It's so easy to do harm.'

She guessed he was really talking about something else and longed to draw the truth out of him, but instinct warned her to go carefully. He'd given her a clue to his fierce self-control, but she knew by now that he would clam up if she pressed him.

And the time was not right. For the moment she must comfort him and ease his mind.

'You didn't do me any harm,' she insisted.

'If I had I'd never forgive myself.'

'But why? I broke into your house. I'm little more than a common criminal. Why aren't you sending for the police?'

'Shut up!' he said, enfolding her in his arms.

He didn't try to kiss her, just sat holding her tightly against him, as if fearing that she might try to escape.

'That's nice,' she murmured. 'Just hold me.'

She felt his lips against her hair, felt the temptation that ran through him, but sensed wryly that he wasn't going to yield to it. He had something else on his mind.

'How badly bruised are you?' he asked.

'A few knocks, nothing much.'

'Let me see.'

He got to work, opening the buttons of her blouse, drawing it off her, removing her bra, but seemingly unaffected by the sight of her bare breasts.

'Lie down so that I can see your back,' he said.

Wondering, she did so, and lay there while he studied her.

'It's not so bad,' she said.

'I'll get a shirt for you to wear tonight.'

'No need. My things are next door. I've been here several days. Nobody saw me because of the shutters. I brought enough food to manage on and crept about. You see, I'm a really dishonest character.'

He groaned. 'And if something had happened to you? If you'd had a fall and been knocked out? You could have died without anyone knowing and lain here for days, weeks. Are you crazy, woman?'

She twisted around and sat up to face him.

'Yes, I think I am,' she agreed. 'I don't understand anything any more.'

He ground his teeth. 'Do I need to explain to you why the thought of your being in danger wrenches me apart? Are you insensitive as well as crazy and stupid?'

'My danger didn't bother you when I was on that boat that overturned.' A thought struck her. 'Unless you didn't know about it.'

'Of course I knew about it. I went to the harbour in case you needed me. I saw you arrive. After that, I knew you were all right.'

'You—?' she echoed slowly.

'The accident was on the news. Of course I went to see how you were. I saw you get off the boat, straight into Nikator's arms. I didn't want to disturb a touching reunion, so I went home.'

'You were there all the time?' she whispered.

'Where the hell would you expect me to be when you were in danger?' he raged. 'What do you think I am? Made of ice?'

Now she was glad of the understanding that was gradually coming to her, and which saved her from misjudging him. Without it she would have seen only his anger, entirely missing the fear and pain which tortured him more because he had no idea how to express them.

'No,' she said helplessly, holding out her arms to him. 'I'd never think that. Oh, I've been so stupid. I shouldn't have let you fool me.'

'What does that mean?' he asked, going into her arms.

'You hide from people. But I won't let you hide from me.'

He looked down at her naked breasts, just visible in the shadowy light. Slowly, he drew his fingertips down one until they reached the nipple, which was already proud and expectant.

'No more hiding,' he murmured.

'There's nowhere to hide from each other,' she said. 'There never was.'

'No, there never was.'

She began to work on his buttons but he forestalled her, undressing quickly, first his jacket, then his shirt. She leaned towards him so that her breasts touched his bare skin, and felt the tremors that possessed his body, guessed that he would have controlled them if he could, for he was still not yet ready to abandon himself. But that control was beyond him, she was delighted to see.

They removed the rest of their clothes, watching each other with brooding possessiveness, taking their time, for this mattered too much to be rushed. He was still fearful lest he hurt her, caressing her gently, almost tentatively, until the deep motion of her chest told him of her mounting impatience.

For too long she'd dreamed of this moment, and nothing was going to deprive her of it now. She kept her hands against his skin, moving them softly to tease him and make sure he continued with what he was doing.

His touch had made her nipples hard and peaked, so that when she leaned against him he drew a long, shaking breath at the impact.

'This is dangerous,' he whispered.

'Who for?' she challenged. 'Not me.'

'Does nothing scare you?'

'Nothing,' she assured him against his lips, 'nothing.'

She released him briefly to finish removing her clothes, and when he had done the same they returned to each other with new fervour. Now she had what she wanted—the sight of him naked and eager for her—and her blood raced at the thought of meeting his eagerness with her own.

His fingers on her skin made it flame with life.

'Yes—' she whispered. 'Yes—yes—I'm here—come here—'

He pressed her gently back against the pillows and began to caress her everywhere—her neck, her waist, her hips. He was taking his time, arousing her slowly, giving her every chance to think if this was really what she wanted. But thinking was the last thing she could do now. Everything in her was focused on one craving—to enjoy the physical release he could give her and discover if it fulfilled all the wild hopes she'd been building up. It would. It *must*.

She caressed him in return, wherever she could reach, frustrated by her limits. She wanted all of him, and even now that he was loving her in the way she most craved, it mysteriously wasn't enough.

Many times she'd wondered about him as a lover. She knew he could be cool, ironic, distant, but with flashes of intensity through which another, wholly different man could be glimpsed. She'd been intrigued by both men, wondering which of them would finally be tempted to her bed, but none of the pictures that came into her head satisfied her. They were incomplete. As a lover he would have yet another identity and she was eager to meet him.

When he finally moved over her she lay back with a sigh, waiting for him. And he was there, inside her, claiming her, completing and fulfilling her. She clasped her legs around him at once, wanting everything, and heard him give a soft growl, as though, by her gesture, she'd told him something he needed to know.

She gasped, rejoicing at the power in his hips as they released the desire that had overcome him, driving her own desire to new heights and making her thrust back at him, digging her fingers cruelly into his flesh.

'Yes—' she whispered. *'Yes!'*

To her delight he was smiling, as though her pleasure gladdened his heart. She'd known he would be a strong lover but her imagination had fallen short of the reality. He took her with power, never seeming to tire, bringing her to the brink several times before taking her over the edge so that his cry joined with hers as they fell together into a bottomless chasm.

For a long time she lay with her eyes closed, enfolded in the world where only pleasure and satisfaction existed. When she opened them again she found that he was lying with his head on her chest, breathing hard. He lifted it slowly and looked at her.

'Are you all right?' he whispered.

'Everything is fine,' she assured him.

Further words failed her. She knew that what had just happened had transformed her life, not merely because he was the most skilled lover she had ever known, but because her heart reached out to him in a way it had never done for any other man. He could possess her and give to her, but what he claimed in return was something she rejoiced to give. By taking from her, he completed her, and that was beyond all words.

He rose and looked at her. Surveying him in return, she smiled. He still wanted her.

Hooking her arm around his neck, she eased herself up, but then winced.

'Did I hurt you?' he demanded, aghast. 'I forgot—'

'So did I,' she promised him. 'I think I'll get in the shower and see what the rest of me looks like.'

He helped her off the bed, which she needed for her exertions seemed to have weakened her. Clinging to him, she went slowly into the bathroom, switching on the lights so that he could see her clearly for the first time, and turning her to look at her back. She heard him draw a sharp breath.

'Nasty,' he said. 'You must have landed on something sharp. I'm so sorry.'

'I can't feel anything,' she said shakily. 'I guess I have too many other things to feel.'

He started the shower and helped her to get under it, soaping her gently, then laving her with water and dabbing her dry. Then he carried her tenderly back to bed and went to fetch her things from the room where she had been camping.

'You wear cotton pyjamas?' he asked as her nightwear came into view.

'What were you expecting? Slinky lingerie? Not when I'm alone. These are practical.'

'I'll see what I can find us to eat,' he said. 'I may have to go out.'

'There's some food in the kitchen. I brought it with me.'

He made them coffee and sandwiches, tending her like a nanny.

'We ought to have talked before anything happened,' he said. 'I didn't want to hurt you.'

She smiled. 'That's easy to say, but I don't think we could have talked before. We had to get past a certain point.'

He nodded. 'But now it's going to be different. I'm going to look after you until you're better.' Tenderly he helped her into her pyjamas, and a thought seemed to strike him. 'How long have you been here?'

'Three days.'

'When did you get back from England?'

'I haven't been to England. What made you think I had?'

'When I found your phone turned off I called the house and spoke to someone who said you'd gone to England with

Nikator. There was a message that neither of you wanted to be disturbed—for quite a while.'

'And you believed that?' she demanded. 'What are you—dead in the head?'

'How could I not believe it? There was nothing to tell me any different. You'd vanished without a trace. Your phone was switched off.'

'I lost it in the water. I've got a new one.'

'How was I supposed to know? You might have gone with him.'

But he knew that wasn't the real reason for his credulity. Nikator's lie had touched a nerve, and that nerve led back to a lack of self-confidence so rare with him that he couldn't cope with it.

Petra was still indignant.

'It wasn't possible,' she fumed. 'It was never possible, and you should have known that.'

'How could I know it when you weren't there to tell me?' he asked reasonably. 'If I didn't think it through properly, maybe it's your fault.'

'Oh, right, fine. Blame me.'

'You left without a word.'

'*I* didn't say a word? What about you? I don't go pestering a man who's shown he doesn't want me.'

'Don't tell me what I want and don't want,' he said with a faint touch of the old ferocity.

'You were pushing me away, you know you were—'

'No, that's not what I—'

'Sending me different signals that I couldn't work out.'

He tore his hair. 'Maybe I couldn't work them out myself. You told me you'd finished with me—'

'I didn't actually say that—'

'The hell you didn't! Have you forgotten some of the

things you said? I haven't. I'll never forget them. I never wanted you to go away. And then—' he took a shuddering breath '—you could have died on that boat, and you might not have been on it if it weren't for me. I just had to know you were safe, but after that—well, you and he seemed so comfortable together.'

'Except that he took the chance to spread lies,' she seethed. 'I was actually beginning to think he might not be so bad after all. I'll strangle him.'

'Leave it for a while,' he soothed. 'Then we'll do it together. But until then you stay in bed until I say you can get up.'

'I'm not fragile,' she protested. 'I won't break.'

'That's my decision. You're going to be looked after.'

'Yes, sir,' she said meekly, through twitching lips.

He threw her a suspicious glance. She retaliated by saluting him.

'I understand, *sir*. I'll just keep quiet and obey, because I'm gonna be looked after whether I like it or not, *sir*!'

He smiled then. 'Oh, I think you might like it,' he said.

'Yes,' she said happily. 'I think I just might.'

That night she slept better than she'd done for weeks. It might be the effect of snuggling down in Lysandros's comfortable bed, waited on hand and foot and told to think of nothing but getting well. Or perhaps it was the blissful sensation of being beside him all night, ordered to, 'Wake me if you need anything.'

Or the moment when she half-awoke in the early hours to find him sitting by the window, and the way he hurried over, saying, 'What is it? What can I do for you?'

This man would astound those who only knew him in the boardroom. His tenderness was real, and so, to her delighted surprise, was his thoughtfulness. He visibly racked his brains to please her, and succeeded because it seemed to matter to him so much. She slipped back contentedly into sleep.

When she awoke the next morning he was gone and the house was silent. Had she misread him? Had he taken what he wanted, then abandoned her to make her suffer for invading his privacy? But, although that fitted with his reputation, she couldn't make herself believe it of the man who'd cared for her so gently last night.

'Aaaaah,' she gasped slowly, rubbing her back as she eased her way out onto the landing.

Downstairs, the front door opened, revealing him. As soon as he saw her at the top of the stairs he hurried up, demanding, 'What are you doing out of bed?'

'I had to get up for a few minutes,' she protested.

'Well, now you can go right back. Come along.'

But once inside the bedroom he pointed her to a chair, saying brusquely, 'Sit there while I remake the bed.'

Gladly she sat down, watching him pull the sheets straight, until finally he came to help her stand.

'I'm just a bit stiff,' she said, clinging to him gladly and wincing.

'You'll be less stiff when I've given you a good rub. I went out for food and I remembered a pharmacy where they sell a great liniment. Get undressed and lie down.'

She did so, lying on her front and gasping as the cool liniment touched her. But that soon changed to warmth as his hand moved here and there over her bruises.

'They seem more tender now than last night,' she mused.

'You should have rested at once,' he told her. 'It's my fault you didn't.'

'Yes,' she remembered, smiling. 'We did something else instead. It was worth it.'

'I'm glad you think so, but I'm not touching you again until you're better.'

'Aren't you touching me now?'

'This isn't the same thing,' he said firmly.

And it wasn't, she thought, frustrated. His fingers moved here and there, sometimes firm, sometimes soft, but tending her, not loving her. There was just one moment when he seemed on the edge of weakening, when his hand lingered over the swell of her behind, as though he was fighting temptation. But then he won the fight and his hand moved firmly on.

She sighed. It wasn't fair.

Later, in the kitchen, she watched as he made breakfast.

'They wouldn't believe it if they could see you now,' she teased.

He didn't need to ask who 'they' were.

'I'm trusting you not to tell them,' he said. 'If you breathe a word of this I'll say you're delusional.'

'Don't worry. This is one secret I'm going to keep to myself. You don't keep any servants here?'

'I have a cleaning lady who comes in sometimes, but I prefer to be alone. Most of the house is shut up, and I just use a couple of rooms.'

'What made you come here now?'

'I needed to think,' he said, regarding her significantly. 'Since we met…I don't know…everything should have been simple…'

'But it never has been,' she mused. 'I wonder if we can make things simple by wanting it.'

'No,' he said at once. 'But if you have to fight—why not? As long as you know what you're fighting for.'

'Or who you're fighting,' she pointed out.

'I don't think there's any doubt about who we'll be fighting,' he said.

'Each other. Yes, it makes it interesting, doesn't it? Exhausting but interesting.'

He laughed and she pounced on it. 'I love it when you laugh. That's when I can claim a victory.'

'You've had other victories that maybe you don't know about.' He added with a touch of self-mockery, 'Or maybe you do.'

'I think I'll leave you to guess about that.'

'It would be a mistake for me to underestimate you, wouldn't it?'

'Definitely.'

Briefly she thought, if only he were always like this, charming and open to her. But she smothered the thought at once. A man who was always charming was like a musician who could only play one note. Eventually it became tedious. Lysandros was fascinating because she never knew who he was going to be from one moment to the next. And nor did he know with her, which kept them both on alert. Could anything be more delightful?

'I'm sorry about last night,' he said.

'I'm not.'

'I mean I'm sorry I didn't wait until you were better.'

'Listen, if you'd had the self-control to wait I'd have taken it as a personal insult. And then I *would* have made you sorry.'

He gave her a curious look. 'I think you will one day, in any case,' he said.

'Perhaps we should both look forward to that.'

She rose, reaching out to take some plates to the sink, but he forestalled her. 'Leave it to me.'

'There's no need to fuss me like an invalid.' She laughed. 'I really can do things for myself.'

His reply was a look of sadness. 'All right,' he said after a moment.

'Lysandros, honestly—'

'I just wish you'd let me give you something—do things for you—'

Heart-stricken, she touched his face, blaming herself for being insensitive.

'I didn't want to be a nuisance,' she whispered. 'You have so many really important things to do.'

He put his arms right around her and drew her close against him.

'There's nothing more important than you,' he said simply.

Later she was to remember the way he'd held her and wonder at it. It hadn't been the embrace of a lover, more the clasp of a refugee clinging onto safety for dear life. He couldn't have told her more clearly that she'd brought something into his life that was more than passion—more life-enhancing while he had it, more soul-destroying if he lost it.

CHAPTER SEVEN

WHEN the washing-up was done Petra asked, 'What are we going to do today?'

'You're going to rest.'

'I think a little gentle exercise will be better for me. I could continue exploring the cellar—'

'No!' This time there was no doubt that he meant it. 'We can have a short outing, an hour on the beach, and lunch, then back here for you to rest.'

'Anything you say.'

Lysandros regarded her cynically.

There was a small car in the garage and he drove them the short distance to the shore, where they found a tiny beach, cut off from the main one and deserted.

'It's private,' Lysandros explained. 'It belongs to a friend of mine. Don't stretch out in this burning sun, not with your fair skin. Do you want to get ill?'

He led her to the rocks, where there was some shade and a small cave that she used for changing. Now she was glad she'd had the forethought to bring a bathing costume when she came to Corfu, meaning to enjoy some swimming while she investigated his house. No chance had occured, but now she changed gladly, longing to feel the sun on her skin, and emerged to find that he'd laid out a large towel for her to lie on. There was even a pillow, making it blissful to lie down, although she hadn't been awake long.

He'd brought some sun lotion to rub in, but was doubtful.

'You shouldn't have this as well as liniment,' he explained. 'We'll leave it for a while, but you stay in the shade. No, don't try to move the towel. Leave it where I put it.'

'Yes, sir. Three bags full, sir.'

He frowned. 'This is something I sometimes hear English people say, but I don't understand it.'

She explained that the words occurred in a nursery rhyme, but he only looked worried.

'You say it to make fun of someone?' he ventured.

'Only of myself,' she said tenderly. 'The mockery is aimed at me, and the way I'm tamely letting you give me orders.'

This genuinely puzzled him. 'But why shouldn't I—?'

'Hush.' She laid a finger over his lips. He immediately kissed it.

'It's for your own good,' he protested. 'To care for you.'

'I know. The joke is that part of me is as much of a sergeant major as you are. I give orders too. But I let you say, "Do this, do that" without kicking your shins as I would with any other man. It's like discovering that inside me is someone else that I've never met before.'

He nodded. 'Yes, that's how it is.'

To complete her protection he'd hired a large parasol. Now he put it up and made sure that she was well covered.

'What about you?' she said. 'You might catch the sun, unless I rub some of that lotion into you.'

Unlike her, he was dark and at less danger from sunburn, but the thought of caressing him under the guise of sun care was irresistible.

'You think I need it?' he asked.

'Definitely.'

He gave her a brief look and lay back beside her so that she could begin work on his chest. He said nothing for a while, just lay still while her fingers worked across his skin, curving to shape the muscles, enjoying herself.

'How did we get here?' he murmured.

'I don't know. We seem to have missed each other so many times. You'd come just so far towards me, then clam up. Everything would be fine between us, then you'd act as though I was an enemy you had to fight off. That night in Athens—'

'I know. I'm sorry about that. I hated myself at the time, but I couldn't stop. You were right to reject me.'

He wasn't fighting her any more and suddenly there was a vulnerable look on his face that she couldn't bear to see. He was powerful and belligerent, but this was her territory where her skills were greater than his, and it was dangerously easy to hurt him.

'We've never understood each other well,' she said gently. 'Perhaps now we have a chance to do that.'

His brow darkened. 'Are you sure you want to try? It might be better not to. I'm bad news. I hurt people. I don't mean to, but often I'm so cut off that I don't realise I'm doing it.'

'You wouldn't be trying to scare me, would you?'

'Warn you. I doubt I could scare you.'

'I'm glad you realise that.'

'So listen to me. Be wise and go now. I'm bad for you.'

'That's all right; I'll just retaliate in kind. When it comes to being bad, you are dealing with an expert.' He started to reply but she silenced him. 'No, I talk, you listen. I've heard what you have to say and I'm not impressed by it. I'm a match for you any day. If we fight, we fight, and you'll come off worst.'

'Oh, will I?' Now his interest was aroused.

'You'd better believe it,' she chuckled. 'Won't that be a new experience for you?'

'A man should be prepared for new experiences. That's how he gets strong and able to achieve victory every time.'

'Every time, hmm?'

'Every time,' he assured her.

'We'll put that to the test. Right now—' she drew back and got to her feet '—I'm going for a swim.'

She was off down the beach before he could get to his feet. By the time he caught her she'd reached the water and hurled herself in. He followed, keeping up with her as she swam out to sea, then getting ahead and stretching out his hands to her. She clasped them, looking up, laughing, rejoicing in the sunlight.

'Steady,' he said, supporting her as she leaned over backwards.

They swam for a while, but she was stiff and as soon as he saw her wince slightly he said, 'Now we're going ashore to have something to eat.'

As they walked up the beach she took the chance to study him. Last night she'd lain with this man, welcomed him inside her, felt a pleasure that only he had ever been able to give, but in the poor light she hadn't seen him properly. Now she looked her fill at his tall muscular body that might have belonged to an athlete instead of a businessman.

Certain moments from their lovemaking came back to her, making her tremble. How easily he'd driven her to new heights, how fierce was the craving he could make her feel, how inspired were the movements of his hands, knowing just where and how to touch her. If she could have had her way she would have pulled him down onto the sand right then. Instead, she promised herself that the wait would not be long.

They found a small restaurant by the sea, and sat where they could watch the waves.

'What happened with the boat?' he asked.

'I don't know really. The weather was fine at first. We went to several caves, didn't find anything. I should never have gone—'

'And you wouldn't have done but for me. If you'd died—'

'That's enough of that.' She stopped him firmly. 'I didn't die. End of story.'

'No,' he said softly. 'It's not the end of the story. We both know that.'

She nodded but said no more.

'After we quarrelled I was sure that we had nothing further to say to each other, but then I heard of your danger and—' he made an agitated gesture '—nothing's been the same since. When I saw you safe the world became bright again, but then there was Nikator. When I heard you'd gone away with him—'

'You should have known better than to believe it.'

'But how could I? You wouldn't believe me when I warned you about him and when I saw you together I thought you'd chosen him over me. I don't really know you at all, except that something here—' he touched his heart '—has always known you.'

'Yes, but that isn't going to make it easy,' she reflected. 'The path led in so many directions that it was confusing, and in the end we stumbled against each other by accident.'

'This meeting was hardly an accident,' he observed lightly. 'You broke into my house.'

'True. I committed a criminal act,' she said, smiling. 'I didn't actually want to. I had planned to ask you to let me explore, but then we quarrelled and—' She gave an eloquent shrug.

He nodded. 'Yes, when you've told a man to go and jump in the lake it would be hard to ask him a favour in the next breath.'

'I'm glad you understand my difficulty. And I couldn't just go tamely away without investigating, could I? Breaking and entering was my only option.'

'But how did you get in? My locks are the most up-to-date.'

Her smile told him that these were minor difficulties, made to be overcome.

'Estelle made a film about organised crime a few years back,' she recalled. 'One of the advisers was a locksmith. I learned a lot from him. He said there was no such thing as a lock that couldn't be picked, even a digital one.'

He regarded her cautiously, not sure whether to believe her. At last he ran a finger gently down her cheek, murmuring, 'So you wouldn't call yourself an honest woman?'

'Honest? Lysandros, haven't you understood yet? I'm a historian. We don't *do* honest, not if it gets in the way. If we want to investigate something, we just go ahead. We break in, we forge papers, we tell lies, we cheat, we do whatever is needed to find out what we need to know. Of course we sometimes get permission as a matter of convenience, but it's not important.'

He grinned. 'I see. And if the owner objects—?'

She regarded him from dancing eyes and leaned forward so that her breath brushed his face.

'Then the owner can take his silly objections and stuff them where the sun doesn't shine,' she murmured.

'I'm shocked.'

'No, you're not. I'll bet it's what you do yourself every day of the week.'

'And I would bet that you could teach me a few new tricks.'

'Any time you like,' she murmured against his lips.

'I was talking about business.'

'I wasn't. Let's go home.'

On the way he stopped off to buy food in quantity, and

Petra realised that he was stocking up for several days. She smiled. That suited her exactly.

The sun was setting as they entered the house and locked the world out. In the shadowy hall he took her into his arms for a long kiss. The feel of his mouth on hers was comforting and thrilling together. He was partly hers and she was going to make him completely hers, as she was already his.

He kissed her neck, moving his lips gently, then resting with his face against her, as though seeking refuge. She stroked his hair until he looked up, meeting her eyes, and together they climbed the stairs to the bedroom.

Last night they had claimed each other with frantic urgency. Tonight they could afford to take their time, confident in each other and their new knowledge of their hearts and what they shared.

At first he moved slowly, cautiously, and she loved him for his care for her. As every garment slipped away he touched her bare flesh as though doubtful that he could take the next step. She undressed him in the same way, eager to discover the body she'd admired on the beach that day.

It didn't disappoint her. He was hard and fit, reminding her of what she'd enjoyed once, making her tremble with the thought of what was to come.

He laid her on the bed and sat for a moment, watching her with possessive eyes.

'Let me look at you,' he whispered.

She was happy for him to do so, knowing that she would please him. A man who'd discovered unexpected treasure might have worn the look she saw on his face. She raised her arms over her head, revelling in flaunting her nakedness for him, knowing that it was worth flaunting.

At last he laid a gentle hand on one breast, relishing the movement as it rose and fell with her mounting desire, then leaning down to circle the nipple with his lips and begin a soft assault. She took a long shuddering breath and immediately arched against him.

'Yes,' she murmured, 'yes—'

'Hush, we don't have to rush.'

How could he say that? she wondered. Already his arousal was fierce and strong, making her reach out with eager exploring fingers. But he was in command of himself, with the power to take his time while he teased and incited her.

'You're a devil,' she whispered.

He didn't reply in words, but he raised his head long enough for his eyes to flash a humorous message, saying, clearer than words, that a devil was what he knew she wanted, and he was going to fulfil her desire.

He increased his devilment, turning up the tension as he got to work on the other breast, moving even more slowly now, making sure she was ready, but she was ahead of him, more than ready, eager and impatient.

'Now,' she breathed. *'Now!'*

He was over her before the words were out, finding the place that was clamouring for him, claiming it with a swift movement that sent her into a frenzy of pleasure.

This was unlike anything that had happened to her before. No man had ever filled her so completely, while still leaving her with a feeling of freedom. She thrust back against him, needing more of him, demanding everything, receiving it again and again.

When it was over she held him tightly, as though needing him for safety in this new world that had opened. But then she realised that there was no safety, for either of them. That was the glory of it.

He raised his head and there was a kind of bafflement in his eyes.

'You—' he said softly, 'you—'

'I know,' she whispered. 'It's the same with me.'

It was as though her words had touched a spring within him, releasing something that brought him peace. He laid his head down on her again, and in a moment he was asleep.

Petra didn't sleep at once. Instead, she lay savouring her joy and triumph, kissing him tenderly, silently promising him everything. Only gradually did she slip away into the happy darkness.

They spent most of the next day in bed, not making love, but cuddling, talking, then cuddling some more in a way that would have been impossible only a short time ago. His body, so perfectly formed and skilled for giving her sexual pleasure, was mysteriously also formed for things cosy, domestic and comforting. It was a mystery, and one she would enjoy solving later.

'I don't know what I'd have done if I'd lost you,' he murmured as they lay curled against each other. 'It felt like being in prison, except that somehow you had the key, and you could help me break out.'

'You kept coming to the edge of escape,' she remembered, 'but then you'd back off again and slam the door.'

'I lost my nerve,' he said with self-contempt. 'I wasn't sure if I could manage, so I'd retreat and lock the doors again. But I couldn't stay in there, knowing you were outside, calling to me that the world was a wonderful place. You saved me the first time; I knew you could save me again.'

'How did I save you?'

His only reply was a long silence, and she felt her heart sink. So often they'd come to the point where he might confide in her, but always his demons had driven him back. This time she'd hoped it might be different, that their loving had given him confidence in her. But it seemed not. Perhaps, after all, nothing had changed.

She'd almost given up hope when Lysandros said in a low voice, 'I never told you why I was in Las Vegas. The fact is

I'd quarrelled with my family. Suddenly it seemed hateful to me that we were always at war about so much. I wanted no more of it. I left home and went out to "live my own life", as I put it. But I got into bad ways. The night we met I'd been like that for two years, and I was headed for disaster if something didn't happen to save me. But something did. I met you.'

'And quarrelled with me,' she said with just a hint of teasing.

'We didn't quarrel,' he said quickly. 'Hell, yes, I suppose we came to the edge of it because I wasn't used to being told a truth I didn't want to hear—that dig about Achilles sulking in his tent.'

'But it wasn't a dig. I was just running over the legend in my usual thoughtless way.'

'I know. You may even have done me a favour.'

Another silence while he fought his inner battle.

'It's all right,' she said. 'Don't tell me anything you don't want to.'

'But I do want to,' he said slowly. 'If you only knew how much.'

She touched his hand again, and felt him squeeze her fingers gratefully.

'That remark got to me,' he said at last. 'I was twenty-three and…I guess, not very mature. I'd left my father to cope alone. You showed me the truth about myself. I did a lot of thinking, and next day I came home and told my father I was ready to take my place in the business. We became a partnership and when he died ten years ago I was able to take over. Thanks to you.'

'Should I be proud of my creation?'

'Do *you* think so?'

'Not entirely. You're not a happy man.'

He shrugged. 'Happiness isn't part of the bargain.'

'I wonder who you struck that bargain with,' she mused. 'Perhaps it was the Furies.'

'No, the Furies are my advance troops that I send into battle. This isn't about my feelings. I do my job. I keep people in work.'

'And so you benefit them. But what about you, yourself, the man?'

His eyes darkened and he seemed to stare into space. 'Sometimes,' he said at last, 'I've felt he hardly exists.'

She nodded. '*He's* an automaton that walks and talks and does what's necessary,' she said. 'But what about *you*?' She laid a soft hand over his heart. 'Somewhere in there, you must exist.'

'Perhaps it's better if I don't,' he said heavily.

'Better for whom? Not you. How can you live in the world and not be part of it?'

He grimaced. 'That's easier than you think. And safer.'

'Safer? You? The man who's supposed to be immortal?'

'*Supposed* to be—'

'Except for that one tiny place on the heel? Shame on you, Achilles. Do you want me to think you're afraid to take the risks that we less glorious mortals take every day?'

He drew a sharp breath and grasped her. 'Oh, you're good,' he said. 'You're clever, cunning, sharp; you know how to pierce a man's heart—'

'You have no heart,' she challenged him. 'At least, not one you care to listen to.'

'And if I listened to it, what do you think it would say to me—about you?'

'I can't tell you that. Only you can know.'

'It will speak in answer to your heart,' he riposted cunningly. 'If I knew what that was saying—'

'Can't you read it?' she whispered.

'Some of it. It laughs at me, almost like an enemy, and yet—'

'Friends laugh too. My heart is your friend, but perhaps an annoying friend. You'll have to be prepared for that.'

'I am, I promise you. Petra—Petra—say you want me.'

'If you haven't worked that out for yourself by now—'

His hands seemed to touch her everywhere at once.

'I hope that means what I think it means,' he growled. 'Because it's too late now.'

She put her arms around his neck. 'Whatever took you so long?'

When she awoke it was early morning and she was alone. Beside her the bed was empty, but the rumpled sheet and pillow showed where he had been. Touching the place, she found that it was still warm.

She sat up listening, but there was only silence. Slipping out of bed, she went to the door, but when she opened it she saw that there was no light on in the bathroom, and some instinct told her that he was in trouble.

She thought she could hear a faint sound from the far end of the corridor. Moving quietly, she followed it to the end, where it turned into another corridor. There she heard the sound again, and this time it sounded like soft footsteps, back and forth. She followed it to the end and waited a moment, her heart beating, before turning the corner.

A short flight of stairs rose before her. At the top stood Lysandros, by the window, looking out onto the world below. He turned, walked back and forth like a man seeing his way in unfamiliar territory, finally coming to a halt in front of a door.

She waited for him to enter the room. Perhaps she could follow him quietly, and so gain a clue to his trouble. But instead he remained motionless for what seemed like an age. Then he leaned against the door, his shoulders sagging in an attitude that suggested he was on the point of collapse. She was about to go to him, offering comfort, when he straightened up and turned around in her direction.

Hurriedly she retreated, and vanished before he could see her. She managed to reach the bedroom without being discovered and was huddled down with her back to him when he came in. She sensed him get in beside her and lean over her, apparently trying to check if she was asleep. She decided to chance it and opened her eyes.

'Hello,' she said, opening her arms to him.

Now, surely, he would come into them and tell her what had happened, because now they were close in hearts and minds and he didn't need to hide things from her.

But, instead, he drew back.

'I'm sorry if I disturbed you,' he said. 'I was just thinking of getting up.'

'You're going to get up now?' she asked slowly.

'Yes, I get stiff lying here all night, but you stay. I'll bring you some coffee later.'

He left the room quickly, leaving her wanting to scream out a protest.

No matter what happiness they seemed to share, beneath it was a torment that hounded him, and which he could not bring himself to share with her. Everything she'd longed for was an illusion. She was still shut out from his deepest heart. She buried her face, and the pillow was wet with her tears.

CHAPTER EIGHT

PETRA wondered how Lysandros would be when they met again at breakfast, whether he would show any awareness of what had happened. But he greeted her cheerfully, with a kiss on the cheek. They might have been any couple enjoying a few days vacation without a care in the world.

'Is there anything you'd like to do?' he asked.

'I'd love to go to Gastouri.'

She was referring to the tiny village where the Achilleion Palace had been built.

'Have you never been before?' he asked in surprise.

'Yes, but it was a hurried visit to get material. Now I'll have time to explore properly.'

And perhaps, she thought, it would help her cope with the sadness of being rejected again.

The village lay about seven miles to the south, built on a slope, with the Palace at the top, overlooking the sea. This was the place that the Empress Elizabeth had built to indulge her passion for the Greek hero, who seemed to have reached out to her over thousands of years. His courage, his complex character, his terrible fate, all were remembered here.

As soon as they entered the gates Petra was aware of the

atmosphere—powerful, vital, yet melancholy, much as Achilles himself must have been.

Just outside the house was the statue of the Empress herself, a tiny figure, looking down with a sad expression, as though all hope had left her.

'She used to annoy my father,' Lysandros said. 'He said she was a silly woman who couldn't pull herself together.'

'Charming.'

'When my mother brought me here he'd insist on coming too, and showing me the things *he* wanted me to remember, like this one.'

He led the way to a tall bronze statue showing Achilles as a magnificent young warrior, wearing a metal helmet mounted with a great feathered crest. On his lower legs was armour, embossed at the kneecaps with snarling lions.

From one arm hung a shield while the other hand held a spear. He stood on a sixteen-foot plinth, looming over all-comers, staring out into the distance.

'Disdainful,' Petra said thoughtfully. 'Standing so far above, he'd never notice ordinary mortals like us, coming and going down here.'

'Perhaps that's how Sisi liked to picture him,' Lysandros suggested with a touch of mischief.

'Sisi knew nothing about it,' Petra said at once. 'After her death the Palace was sold to a man, and *he* put this statue here.'

He grinned. 'I might have guessed you'd know that.'

'So that's who your father wanted you to be,' she reflected, straining her head back to look up high to Achilles' face.

'Nothing less would do for him. There's also the picture inside which he admired.'

The main hall was dominated by a great staircase, at the top of which was a gigantic painting depicting a man in a racing chariot, galloping at full speed, dragging the lifeless body of his enemy in the dirt behind.

'Achilles in triumph,' Petra said, 'parading his defeated enemy around the walls of Troy.'

'That was how a man ought to be,' Lysandros mused. 'Because if you didn't do it to them, they would do it to you. So I was raised being taught how to do it to them.'

'And do you?'

'Yes,' he replied simply. 'If I have to, otherwise I wouldn't survive, and nor would the people who work for me.'

'Parading lifeless bodies?' she queried.

'Not literally. My enemies are still walking about on earth, trying to destroy me. But if you've won, people have to know you've won, and the lengths you were prepared to go to. That way they learn the lesson.'

For a moment his face frightened her, not because it displayed harshness or cruelty, but because it displayed nothing at all. He was simply stating a fact. Victory had to be flaunted or it was less effective, and she could see that he didn't really understand why this troubled her.

They moved on through the building, looking at the friezes and murals, the paintings and statues all telling of another world, yet one that still reached out to touch this one. Lysandros might speak wryly of his mother's fascination with the legendary Achilles, yet even he felt the story's power over him.

Heroism was no longer simple as in those days, but he'd been born into a society that expected him to conquer his enemies and drag them behind his chariot wheels. The past laid its weight on him, almost expecting him to live two lives at once, and he knew it. Fight it as he might, there were times when the expectations almost crushed him.

If she'd doubted that, she had the proof when they moved

back into the garden and went to stand before the great statue depicting Achilles' last moments. He lay on the ground, trying to draw the arrow from his heel, although in his heart he knew it was hopeless. His head was raised to the heavens and on his face was a look of despair.

'He's resigned,' Lysandros said. 'He knows there's no escaping his destiny.'

'Then perhaps he shouldn't be so resigned,' Petra said at once. 'You should never accept bad luck as inevitable. That's just giving in.'

'How could he help it? He knew his fate was written on the day he was born. It was always there on his mind, the hidden vulnerability. Except that in the end it wasn't hidden, because someone had known all the time. None of us hide our weaknesses as well as we think we do.'

'But perhaps,' she began tentatively, 'if the other person was someone we didn't have to be afraid of, someone who wouldn't use it against us—'

'That would be paradise indeed,' Lysandros agreed. 'But how would you know, until it was too late?'

They strolled for a while in the grounds before he said, 'Is there any more you need to see here, or shall we go?'

On the way home his mood seemed to lighten. They had a cheerful supper, enlivened by an argument about a trivial point that he seemed unable to let go of, until he covered his eyes with his hands, in despair at himself.

'It doesn't matter, does it?' he groaned. 'I know it doesn't matter and yet—'

'You're a mess,' she said tenderly. 'You don't know how to deal with people—unless they're enemies. You deal with *them* well enough, but anyone else—you're left floundering. You know what you need?'

'What's that?'

'Me. To put you on a straight line and keep you there.'

'Where does this line lead?'

'Back to me, every time. So make up your mind to it; I'm taking charge.'

He regarded her for a moment, frowning, and she wondered if she'd pushed his dictatorial nature too far. But then the frown vanished, replaced by a tender smile.

'That's all right, then,' he said.

She smiled in a way that she could see he found mystifying. Good. That suited her perfectly.

Quickly she reached into her pocket, drew out a small notebook and pencil that never left her, then began counting on her fingers and making notes.

'What are you doing?' he demanded.

'Calculating. Do you know it's exactly eighteen hours and twenty-three minutes since you made love to me?' She sighed theatrically. 'I don't know. Some men are all talk.'

Before he could think of an answer, she rose and darted away.

'Hey, where are you going?'

'Where do you think?' she called back over her shoulder from halfway up the stairs.

He managed to pass her on the stairs and reach the bedroom first.

'Come here,' he said, yanking her close and holding her tightly, without gentleness. *'Come here.'*

It was less a kiss than an act of desperation. She knew that as soon as his lips touched hers, not tenderly but with a ferocity that mirrored her own. They had shared kisses before, but this was a step further. In the past she'd been struggling with her own reaction, and doubtful of his. But the previous two times they'd made love had told each of them something about the other, and where they were going together.

Now there were no doubts on either side, no room for

thoughts or even emotions. They wanted each other as a simple physical act, free of everything but the need for satisfaction.

His mouth seemed to burn hers while his tongue invaded her, demanding, asking no quarter and giving none. His urgency thrilled her for it matched her own, but she wouldn't let him know that just yet. She had another plan in mind.

'Mmm, just as I hoped,' she murmured.

He ground his teeth. 'You pulled my strings and I jumped, didn't I?'

''Fraid so. And you have another problem now.'

'Surprise me.'

'I'm a horrible person. In fact I'm just horrible enough to get up and walk away right now.'

His hands tightened on her in a grip of steel. *'Don't even think about it.'*

She began to laugh with delight, revelling in the ruthless determination with which he held her, threw her onto her back and invaded her like a conqueror. She was still laughing when her explosion of pleasure sent the world into a spin.

Afterwards he looked down at her, gasping and frenzied.

'You little—*it's not funny!'*

'But it is funny. Oh, my darling, you're so easily fooled.'

He began to move inside her again, slowly, making her wait but leaving her in no doubt that he had the strength and control to prolong the moment.

'Were you expecting this too?' he whispered.

'Not exactly expecting, but I was hoping—oh, yes, I was hoping you'd do just what you're doing now—and again—and again—oh, darling, *don't stop!'*

She ceased to be aware of time, losing track of how often he brought her to climax. It didn't matter. All that mattered was that he'd transported her to another world, while giving her the vital feeling that she too had transported him. Whatever happened to them happened together, and she cared about nothing else.

When he finally managed to speak it was with ironic humour.

'I did it again, didn't I? Danced to your tune. Is there any way I can get one step ahead of you?'

She seemed to consider this. 'Probably not. But I'd hate you to stop trying.'

Now it was his turn to laugh. She felt it against her before she heard it, and her soul rejoiced because it was through laughter that she could reach him.

The next few days were hazy. They spent much of the time out, wandering the island or lazing on the beach, their evenings indoors, talking with a freedom which once would have been impossible. They spent the nights in each other's arms.

She knew it couldn't last for ever. For now they were living in a world apart, where each of them could yield to the new personality the other could evoke. He could doff his harsh exterior, emerge from the prison cell where his heart normally lived, and let her see the side of him that was charming and outgoing.

But it was unreal. Such perfect happiness could never last unchallenged. Sooner or later she must face the part of him that remained hidden from her, or retire in defeat because he wouldn't allow her in.

She'd never told him of the night she'd followed him to the distant room. Once she slipped upstairs to try the door and, as she'd expected, found it locked. In her mind it came to symbolise the fact that she still hadn't gained entry into the deepest heart of him. Despite their happiness, she wondered if she ever would.

One night she awoke to find herself alone again. The door was open and from a distance she thought she could hear sounds. Quickly she scrambled out into the corridor and was just in time to see Lysandros turning the corner. He walked in a slow, dazed manner, as though he was sleepwalking.

When she reached the little staircase he was just standing at the top. He approached the door slowly, then, before her horrified eyes, he began to ram his head against it again and again, as though by seeking pain he could blot out unbearable memories.

Suddenly she was back on the roof all those years ago and he was in her arms, banging his head against her, seeking oblivion from misery too great to be borne. And she knew that fifteen years had changed nothing. In his heart he was the same young man now as then.

She would have run to him, but he stopped suddenly and turned, leaning back against the door. Through the window the moonlight fell on his face, showing her a depth of agony that shocked her.

He didn't move. His eyes were closed, his head pressed back against the door, his face raised as though something hovered in the darkness above him. As she watched, he lifted his hands and laid them over his face, pressing them close as though he could use them as a shield against the Furies that pursued him. But the Furies were inside him. There was no escape.

Wisdom told her to retreat and never let him know that she'd seen him like this, but she couldn't be wise now. He might try to reject her, but she must at least offer him her comfort.

She moved the rest of the way quickly and quietly, then reached up to draw his hands away. He started, gazing at her with haggard eyes that saw a stranger.

'It's all right; it's only me,' she whispered.

'What are you doing here?'

'I came because you need me—yes, you do,' she added quickly before he could speak. 'You think you don't need anyone, but you need me because I understand. I know things that no one else knows, because you shared them with me long ago.'

'You don't know the half of it,' he whispered.

'Then tell me. What's in that room, Lysandros? What draws you here? What do you see when you go inside?'

His reply startled her. 'I never go inside.'

'But…then why…?'

'I don't go in because I can't bear to. Each time I come here, hoping to find the courage to enter, but that never happens.' He gave a mirthless snort of laughter. 'Now you know. *I'm a coward.*'

'Don't—'

'I'm a coward because I can't face her again.'

'Is she in there?' Petra asked.

'She always will be. You think I'm mad? Well, perhaps. Let's see.'

He opened his hand, revealing the key, allowing her to take it and put it in the lock. Turning it slowly, she pushed on the door. It stuck as though protesting after being closed for so long, but then a nudge opened it and she stood on the threshold, holding her breath, wondering fearfully what she would find.

At first she could see very little. Outside the dawn was breaking, but the shutters were still closed and only thin slivers of light managed to creep in. By their faint glow she realised that this room had been designed as a celebration of love.

The walls were covered in paintings depicting gods, goddesses and various Greek legends. Incredibly, Petra thought she recognised some of them.

'These pictures are famous,' she murmured. 'Botticelli, Titian—'

'Don't worry, we didn't steal them,' Lysandros said. 'They're all copies. One of my mother's ancestors wanted to "make a figure" in the world. So he hired forgers to go all over Europe and copy the works of great artists—paintings, statues. You'll probably recognise the statues of Eros and Aphrodite as well.'

'The gods of love,' she whispered.

'His wife directed matters, and had this room turned into a kind of temple.'

'It's charming,' Petra said. 'Had they made a great love match?'

'No, he married the poor woman for her money, and this was her way of trying to deny it.'

'How sad.'

'Love often is sad when you get past the pretty lies and down to the ugly truth,' he said in a flat voice.

But now she scarcely heard him. Disturbing impressions were reaching her. Something was badly wrong, but she wasn't sure what. Then she drew closer to a statue of Eros, the little god of love, and a chill went through her.

'His face,' she murmured. 'I can't see, but surely—'

With a crash Lysandros threw open the shutters, filling the room with pale light. Petra drew a sharp, horrified breath.

Eros had no face. It looked as if it had been smashed off by a hammer. His wings, too, lay on the floor.

Now she could look around at the others and see that they were all damaged in a similar way. Every statue had been attacked, every painting defaced.

But the worst of all was what had happened to the bed. It had been designed as a four-poster but the posts too had been smashed, so that the great canopy had collapsed onto the bed, where it lay.

Someone had attacked this temple to love in a frenzy, and then left the devastation as it was, making no attempt to clear up. Now she could see the thick dust. It had been like this, untouched, for a long, long time. That was as terrible as the damage with its message of soul-destroying bitterness.

'You asked if she were in here,' Lysandros said. 'She's been here since the night I brought her to this house, to this room, and we made love. She'll always be here.'

'Was she here when—?'

'When I did this? When I took an axe and defaced the statues and the pictures, smashed the bed where we'd slept, wanting to wipe out every trace of what I'd once thought was love? No, she wasn't here. She'd gone. I didn't know where she was and after that—I didn't find her until she died, far away.'

He turned to the wrecked bed, gazing at it bleakly as though it held him transfixed. Shivers went through Petra as she realised that he'd spoken no more than the truth. His dead love was still present, and she always would be. She followed him through every step of his life, but she was always here, in this house, in this room, in his heart, in his nightmares.

'Come away,' she said. 'There's nothing here any more.'

It wasn't true. In this room was everything that was terrible, but she wouldn't admit that to him, lest her admission crush him further. She drew him to the door and locked it after them. She knew it would take more than a locked door to banish this ghost from his dark dreams, but she was determined to do it.

He's got me now, she told the lurking presence in her mind. *And I won't let you hurt him any more.*

She didn't speak to Lysandros again, just led him back to their bed and held him in her arms.

At last some life seemed to return to Lysandros and he roused himself to speak.

'Since we've been here together, I've found myself going more and more to that room, hoping that I could make myself enter and drive the ghost away.'

'Perhaps I can help you do that,' she suggested.

'Perhaps. I've resisted it too long.'

'Am I something you need to resist?' she whispered.

He took so long to reply that she thought he wasn't going to say anything, but at last he spoke as though the words were dragged out of him by pincers.

'From the first evening you have filled me with dread,' he said slowly. 'With dread—with fear. There! That's the truth. Despise me if you will.'

'I could never despise you,' she hastened to say. 'I just can't think of any reason why you should be afraid of me.'

'Not of you, but of the way you made me feel. In your presence my defences seemed to melt away. I felt it when we met at the wedding. When I discovered that you were the girl on the roof in Las Vegas I was glad, because it seemed to explain why I was drawn to you. We'd been practically childhood friends so naturally there was a bond. That's what I told myself.

'But then we danced, and I knew that the bond was something far more. I left the wedding early to escape you, but I called you later that day because I had to. Even then I couldn't stay away from you because you had an alarming power, one I shied away from because I'd never met it before and I knew I couldn't struggle against it.

'Do you remember the statue we saw in the Achilleion Palace? Not the first one where Achilles was in all his glory, but the second one, where he was on the ground, trying to remove the arrow, knowing that he couldn't? Did you see his face, upturned to the sky, begging help from the gods because he knew that this was stronger than him and only divine intervention could save him from its power?'

'But he was fighting death,' Petra reminded him. 'Do I represent death?'

He smiled faintly and shook his head.

'No, but you represent the defeat of everything I believed was necessary to keep me strong. The armour that kept me at a cautious distance from other people, the watchfulness that never let me relax, so that I was always ahead of the game and all the other players. In your presence, all of that vanished. I implored the gods to return my strength so that I could be as safe against you as I was against everyone else, but they didn't listen—possibly because they knew I didn't really mean it.

'Your power over me came from something I'd never considered before. It wasn't sex, although there was that too. Lord, how I wanted to sleep with you, possess you! It drove me half demented, but I could cope with that. It was something else, much more alarming.'

'I know,' she said. 'I could make you laugh. I've always loved doing that, not because it gave me power but because I hoped it might make you happy.'

'It did, but it also alarmed me because it meant I was vulnerable to you as to nobody else in the world, man or woman. So I departed again. This time I went away for days, but then I began to worry that you might have returned to England, and I discovered I didn't want that after all. I was acting like a man with no sense, wanting this, wanting the opposite, not knowing what I wanted—like a man in love, in fact. So I called you.'

'I was with Nikator,' she remembered. 'He guessed it was you and warned me against you.'

'He was right.'

'I know he was. I never doubted that for a moment. Do you think I care what that silly infant thinks, as long as you come back to me?'

'When I saw you again I knew I couldn't have stayed away any longer,' he said, 'but I also knew I'd come back to danger. I was no longer master of myself, and that control—that mastery—has been the object of my life. I understood even then that I couldn't have both it and you, but it's not until now—'

It was only now that he'd brought himself to face the final

decision, and for a moment she still wasn't sure which way it would go. There was some terrifying secret that haunted him, and everything would depend on what happened in the next few minutes.

Suddenly she was afraid.

CHAPTER NINE

At last he began to speak.

'It started in my childhood with my mother's fantasies about Achilles and his hidden vulnerability. I understood the point about keeping your secrets to yourself, but in those days it was only theory, little more than a game. I was young, I had more money than was good for me, I felt I could rule the world. I fancied myself strong and armoured, but in truth I was wide open to a shrewd manipulator.'

'Is that what *she* was?' Petra asked.

'Yes, although it wasn't so much her as the men behind her. Her name was Brigitta. She was a great-niece of Homer, not that I knew that until later. We met by chance—or so I thought—on a skiing holiday. In fact she was an excellent skier, but she concealed that, just kept falling over, so I began to teach her and somehow we fell over a lot together.

'Then we abandoned skiing and went away to be by ourselves. I was in heaven. I didn't know any girl could be so lovely, so sweet, so honest—'

He drew a ragged breath and dropped his head down onto his chest. He was shaking, and she wondered with dismay if this was only memory. After all these years, did some part of his love still survive to torment him?

She reached out to touch him but stopped at the last minute and let her hand fall away. He didn't seem to notice.

After a while he began to speak again.

'Of course I was deceiving myself. It had all been a clever trap. She was thrown into my path on purpose so that I could make a fool of myself over her. Even when I discovered who she was I didn't have the wit to see the plot. I believed her when she said she'd concealed her background because she was truly in love with me and didn't want me to be suspicious. Can you imagine anything so stupid?'

'It's not stupid,' Petra protested. 'If you really loved her, of course you wanted to think well of her. And you must have been so young—'

'Twenty-one, and I thought I knew it all,' he said bitterly.

'How old was she?'

'Nineteen. So young; how could I possibly suspect her? Even when I found out she was using a false name, that she'd engineered our meeting—even then I believed that she was basically innocent. I *had* to believe it. She was the most beautiful thing that had ever happened to me.'

She could have wept for the boy he'd been then. To cling to his trust in the face of the evidence suggested a naïvety that nobody meeting him now would ever believe.

'What happened?' she asked.

'We planned to marry. Everyone went wild—the two foes putting their enmity aside to join forces and present a united front to the world. My father advised me to delay; he was uneasy. I wouldn't listen. We came here to be alone together and spent the summer living in this house. I wouldn't have thought that anyone could be as happy as I was in those weeks.'

His mouth twisted in a wry smile.

'And I'd have been right not to believe it. It was all an illusion, created by my own cowardly refusal to face the fact that she was a spy. She didn't learn much, but enough for the Lukas family to pip us to the post on a lucrative contract. It was obvious that the information must have come from her, and that she'd listened in to a telephone conversation I'd had and managed to see some papers. She denied it at first, but there was simply no other way. I turned on her.'

'Well, naturally, if you felt betrayed—'

'No, it was worse than that. I was cruel, brutal. I said such things—she begged my forgiveness, said she'd started as a spy but regretted it in the end because she came to love me truly.'

'Did you believe her?' Petra asked.

'I didn't dare. I sneered at her. If she truly regretted what she'd done, why hadn't she warned me? She said she tried to back out but Nikator threatened to tell me everything. But he promised to let her off if she did one last job, so that's what she did.'

'But Nikator must have been little more than an child in those days,' Petra protested.

'He was twenty. Old enough to be vicious.'

'But could he have organised it? Would he have known enough?'

'No. There was another man, a distant cousin called Cronos, who hadn't been in the firm more than a couple of years and was still trying to make his mark. Apparently he was a nasty piece of work, and he and Nikator hit it off well, right from the start. People who knew them said they moved in the same slime. Cronos set it up and used Nikator as front man.'

'Cronos set it up?' she echoed. 'Not Homer?'

'No, to do him justice, he's a fairly decent man, a lot better than many in this business. The story is that after the whole thing exploded Homer tore a strip off Cronos and told him to get out if he knew what was good for him. At any rate Cronos vanished.

'Obviously, I don't know the details of any family rows, but my impression is that Homer was shocked by Nikator's behaviour. Being ruthless in business is one thing, but you don't involve innocent young girls. But Nikator had come down hard on Brigitta when she tried to get free. He bullied her into "one last effort", and she thought if she did that it would be over.'

'No way,' Petra said at once. 'Once he had a blackmail hold over her he'd never have let it go.'

'That's what I think too. She was in his power; I should have seen that and helped her. Instead, I turned on her. You can't imagine how cruelly I treated her.'

But she could, Petra thought. Raised with suspicion as his constant companion, thinking he'd found the love and trust that could make his life beautiful, he'd been plunged back into despair and it had almost destroyed him. He'd lashed out with all the vigour of a young man, and in the process he'd hurt the one person he still loved.

'I said such things,' he whispered. 'I can't tell you the things I said, or what they did to her—'

'She'd deceived you.'

'She was a child.'

'So were you,' she said firmly. 'Whatever happened to her, *they* were responsible, the people who manipulated her. Not you.'

'But I should have saved her from them,' he said bleakly. 'And I didn't. We had a terrible scene. I stormed out of the house, saying I hated the sight of her and when I returned she'd vanished. She left me a letter in which she said that she loved me and begged my forgiveness, but there was nothing to tell me where she'd gone.'

Petra made no sound, but her clasp on him tightened.

'I couldn't—wouldn't believe it at first,' he went on in a voice that was low and hoarse. 'I went through the house calling her name. I was sure she had to be hiding somewhere, waiting for a sign from me. I cried out that we would find our way somehow, our love was worth fighting for.'

And after each call he'd stood and listened in the silence. Petra could see it as clearly as if she'd walked the house with that devastated young man. She heard him cry, *'Brigitta!'* again and again, waited while he realised that there would be no answering call, and felt her heart break with his as the truth was forced on him.

And she saw something else that he would never speak of—the moment when the boy collapsed in sobs of despair.

'What did you do after that?' she asked, stroking his hair.

'I believed I could find her and still make it right. I set detectives on her trail. They were the best, but even they couldn't find her. She'd covered her tracks too well. I tried the few who remained of her family in another country, but they weren't close and she hadn't been in touch with them. I tried Nikator. There was just a chance that he knew something, but I'm convinced he didn't. I scared him so badly that he'd have told me if he could.

'In the end I faced facts. A woman who could escape so completely must have been very, very determined to get well away from me. But I didn't stop. Months passed, but I told them to keep looking because I couldn't face the prospect of never seeing or talking to her again. I had to ask her forgiveness, do what I could to make it right.

'At last I got a message from a man who said he thought he might have found her, but it was hard to be sure because she couldn't talk and just sat staring into space all the time. I went to see her and found—' He shuddered.

Petra didn't make the mistake of speaking. She simply sat with him in her arms, praying that her love would reach him and make it possible for him to confront the monster.

'I found her in a shabby room in a back street, miles away,' he managed to say at last. 'The door was locked. The last time anyone had gone in there she'd been so frightened that she'd locked it after them. I kicked it open and went in.

'She was sitting up on a bed in the corner, clutching something in her arms as though she had to protect it. She screamed at the sight of me and backed away as though I was an enemy. Maybe that's how I looked to her then. Or maybe she just didn't know me.'

Another silence, in which she felt his fingers tighten on her arm, release her and tighten again.

'At last all the fight seemed to go out of her. She sagged against the wall and I managed to get close and look at what she was holding.'

His grip was agonisingly tight. Petra closed her eyes, guessing what the bundle had been, and praying to be wrong.

'It was a dead baby,' Lysandros said at last.

'Oh, no,' Petra whispered, dropping her head so that her lips lay against his hair.

'It was premature. She'd hidden her pregnancy and had no proper medical attention, so she gave birth alone. Then she just sat clutching the child and not letting anyone near her. She'd been like that for days, shivering, starving, weeping.

'I begged her to calm down, told her it was me, that I loved her, I'd never harm her, but she told me to go away because she had to feed the baby. By that time he must have been dead for days. He was cold in her arms.

'The people who owned the house were decent and kindly, but they couldn't cope. I had her moved to hospital, ordered the best attention for her, said I'd pay for everything— whatever money could buy, I'd give her.' He said the last words with bitter self-condemnation.

'I went to see her every day in the hospital, always thinking that the care she was receiving would soon take effect, she would become herself again, and we could talk. But it didn't happen. As she became physically stronger her mind seemed to retreat further into a place where I couldn't follow, and I understood that she wanted it that way. But still I waited, hoping she'd recover and we could find each other again.

'Then she had a heart attack, apparently an adverse reaction to a drug she'd been given, but the doctors told me that she wasn't fighting for life. Her will had gone, and it was only a matter of time. I sat beside her, holding her hand, praying for her to awaken. When she did I told her that I loved her and begged her forgiveness.'

'Did she forgive you?' Petra asked quietly.

'I don't know. She only said one thing. By that time she'd accepted that the child was dead and she begged me to make sure he was buried with her. I gave her my word and, when the time came, I kept it. She's buried with our baby in her arms.'

'She must have recognised you to ask such a thing,' Petra said.

'I've told myself that a thousand times, but the truth is that she might have said it to anyone she thought had the power to ensure that it happened. I've tried to believe that she forgave me, but why should I? What right do I have after what I did? I terrified her into running away and hiding from the world when she desperately needed help.

'What kind of life did she have? The doctors told me she was severely undernourished, which had damaged the child, hence the premature birth—and death—of my son.'

'You have no doubt that—?'

'That he was mine? None. She must have been about a month pregnant when we parted. They were very tactful. They offered me a test, to be sure, but I refused. Such a test implied a doubt that dishonoured her. She was carrying my son when I abandoned her.'

'But you didn't throw her out,' Petra protested.

'No, I wanted her to stay here until I could arrange our breakup to look civilised in the eyes of the world,' he said savagely. 'And then, fool that I was, I was surprised when I came back and found her gone. Of course she fled. She looked into the future I'd mapped out and shuddered. I didn't throw her out, but I drove her out with coldness and cruelty.

'If I'd known—everything would have been different, but I made her feel that she had no choice but to run away from me. So there was nobody to help her when she knew about her condition. She faced everything alone, and they both died.

'I was with her to the last. She died in my arms, while I prayed for a word or a look to suggest that she knew me. But there was nothing. She'd gone beyond my reach and all I could do was hold her while she slipped away, never knowing that I was begging her forgiveness. I destroyed her life, I destroyed her last moment, I destroyed our child—'

'But it wasn't—'

'It's my fault—don't you understand? *I killed them, both of them.* I killed them as surely as if I'd—'

'No,' she said fiercely. 'You mustn't be so hard on yourself.'

'But I must,' he said bleakly. 'If I'm not hard on myself, who will be? How many times since then have I gone to her tomb and stood there, watching and waiting for something that's never going to happen?'

'Where is her tomb?'

'Here, in the garden. I had the ground consecrated and got the priest to come and bury them both at the dead of night. Then I covered the place so that nobody can find it by accident.

'Then I had to decide what to do with myself. I looked at what this kind of life had made of me, and I hated it. I told my father I was finished with it all, and took the next plane out of Greece, trying to escape what I'd done, what I'd turned into.

'When you and I met, I'd been on the run for two years.' He gave a brief bark of laughter. 'On the run. Like a criminal. That's how I felt. I went to Monte Carlo, to New York, Los Angeles, London, Las Vegas—anywhere I could live what they call "the high life", which is another way of saying I indulged myself in every despicable way. I drank too much, gambled too much, slept around too much, all because I was trying to escape myself. But at the end, there was always a menacing figure waiting for me at the end of the road. And it was me.

'Then, one night in Las Vegas—well, you know the rest. You showed me to myself in a light I couldn't bear, and I returned to Greece the next day.'

'It wasn't just me,' Petra said. 'You were ready to see things differently or I couldn't have had any effect.'

'Maybe. I don't know.' He gave her a faint smile. 'Part of me prefers to give you the credit—my good angel, who stopped me going even further astray the first time and now—'

'Now?' she asked cautiously.

'I'm not blind, Petra. I know about myself. I'm not a man anyone in their right mind could want to meet. I scare people, and that's been fine up to now. It suited me. But you showed me the truth then, and somehow you've done it again. For years I've sheltered deep inside myself because that way I felt safer. I keep people at a distance because if you don't let yourself need anyone, nobody can hurt you.

'But I can't keep you at a distance because you've been in there—' he touched his heart '—for a long time. I've never told anyone else what I've told you tonight, and I never will. Now you know all my secrets and I'm glad of it, for a burden is gone from me.'

He rested his face against her and she dropped her head, while her tears fell on him.

They slept for a while and awoke in each others' arms, to

find daylight flooding into the room. Anxiously, Petra looked at his face but was reassured. He was smiling, relaxed.

'No regrets?' she asked softly.

He shook his head. 'None with you. Never. Come with me.'

They dressed and he took her hand, leading her downstairs and out of the house.

She'd briefly glimpsed the garden from an upstairs window and seen that it was mainly a wilderness. Everything was overgrown, and now she thought she knew why.

He led her to a distant place under the trees and removed some branches and leaves. Beneath them was a stone in which were carved a few simple words and dates. He had hidden Brigitta and her child away from the world, protecting them as best he could. Without asking, Petra knew that nobody else had ever seen this place.

'So many times I've stood here and begged her forgiveness,' he said. 'What should I tell her about you?'

Her grandfather had once told her that no true Greek was ever completely free of the past. Now Lysandros, this modern man, at home in the harsh world of multibillion dollar business, spoke like an ancient Greek who felt the River Styx swirl around his feet and, beyond it, Hades, the other world, where souls still suffered and communicated with the living.

Could it be true? Was Brigitta there now, gazing at him across the waters, drawing him back, crying that he was hers alone and they should be together for all eternity?

No! She wouldn't allow it.

'You don't have to tell her anything about me,' she said. 'She knows that I love you, just as she does. And, because of that love, she forgives you. Don't forget that where she is now, she understands everything she didn't understand before and she wants your suffering to end.'

It touched her heart to see the relief that came into his face, as though anything said by herself could be trusted, however strange or outrageous it might sound to anyone else.

They walked slowly back into the house and upstairs. Now he kissed her softly, almost tentatively, letting her know that this was different from any other time. They had crossed a boundary of love and trust, and the way ahead was changed for ever.

'Mine,' he whispered, 'all mine.'

'Yours as long as you want me,' she whispered back.

'That will be for ever.'

'And are you mine?' she asked.

'I think I've been yours since the first moment. In my heart I always knew. It just took this long to admit it.'

They lay down, holding each other, touching gently, eager to explore yet unwilling to hurry. Taking their time was a tribute that they owed to each other and they paid it in full. He sought the places where her bruises had been worst, laying his lips over them in care and comfort.

'I'm fine now,' she said. 'You've looked after me so well.'

'And I always will,' he vowed.

His fingers played in a leisurely way over her breasts, first one, then the other, almost as if he were discovering them for the first time, wondering at their beauty. At last he laid his face against them and she felt his tongue, softly caressing. Tremors went through her. New life invaded her body.

She began to run her own hands over him, exploring and teasing him, rejoicing at the suppressed groan that came from him.

'You do your magic,' he breathed. 'Where does it come from? Are you one of the sirens?'

'Do you want me to be?'

'Only for me. No other man must hear that siren-song. And I must hear it for ever.'

She turned, pressing him gently onto his back and lying across him so that her peaked nipples brushed him lightly.

'But they did hear it for ever,' she said, inviting him further into the fantasy. 'Those doomed sailors knew it would be the last sound they ever heard. Did they follow it willingly?'

This was the question he'd asked himself many times but always in solitude. Now, in her arms, he knew the answer.

'Willingly,' he agreed, 'because at the last nothing else mattered. Nothing else—ever—but to follow that song wherever it led.'

She smiled down at him. 'An adventurous man,' she mused. 'That's what I like. I'm going to take you to such places—where no one's ever been before—'

'Wherever it leads,' he murmured. 'As long as it leads us together.'

When he turned again to bring her beneath him she went gladly, opening for him in warmth and welcome, feeling herself become complete, and then complete again as they climaxed together.

'No,' she begged as it ended. 'Don't leave me.'

'I shall never leave you,' he said, changing her meaning. 'My body will never leave you and nor will my heart. I'm yours. Do you understand that? Yours for always.'

'My darling—'

'I wish I could find the words to tell you what it means to me to have found someone I need never doubt. It's more than happiness. It's like being set free.'

'Dearest, be careful,' she said worriedly. 'I'm human, not perfect.'

'Rubbish, you *are* perfect,' he said, laughing.

'I'll never knowingly betray you, but I might make some silly human mistake. Please, please don't think me better than I am, in case you end up thinking me worse than I am.'

'It wouldn't be possible to think you better than you are,' he said. 'You are perfect. You are honest and true, and divinely inspired to be the one person on earth who can keep me safe and happy.'

There was no middle way with this man, she realised. It was all or nothing, with no reservations. The heartfelt simplicity with which he placed himself and his fate in her hands made her want to weep. And silently she prayed that he might never be disappointed in her, for she knew it would destroy him.

CHAPTER TEN

LYSANDROS awoke in the darkness to find Petra watching him.

'What is it?' he asked. 'Something on your mind? Tell me.' When she still hesitated he sat up and slipped an arm around her. 'Tell me,' he repeated. 'You've always wanted me to talk, but how often do you confide in me?'

When she didn't answer he said, 'It has to work each way, you know. If you don't honour me with your confidence, what am I to think?'

'All right, I will,' she said slowly.

'But it's hard, isn't it?'

'Yes, because I've never really explained it before. There was nobody to explain to. You asked me if I was yours. In fact I'm yours more than you know.'

He thought for a moment. 'You mean something special by that, don't you?'

'Yes. There are things I couldn't tell you because they might have been a burden on you.'

'You? A burden? That isn't possible.'

'If you knew how much I depend on you, you might find it a weight.'

'Now you're humouring me. Isn't it me clinging to you because I find in you what I can find in nobody else?'

'I hope you do, but it's mutual and I couldn't admit that before. But, since we've found each other, maybe I can.'

He touched her chin, turning it gently towards him so that he could regard her intently. Now she had all his attention. Something in her voice told him this was vital.

'You're the first person I've ever really mattered to,' she said simply.

'Your mother—'

'Estelle's a darling but I've never figured high on her list of priorities. She'd have loved a pet cat just as much. She's always been dashing off here and there, leaving me with other people, and I didn't mind because the other people were my grandparents and I loved them. But that was pure luck. If we hadn't been lucky enough to have found them, I sometimes wonder what she'd have done.

'My grandparents loved me, but each came first with the other. That's as it should be, but when she died I knew he wouldn't be long following.'

'There must have been men who wanted you,' he observed.

'Well, they wanted something. Maybe it was me, maybe it was what I brought with me—money, a glamorous background. It left me rather cynical, and I kind of hoisted the cynicism into place as a defence, rather like Achilles kept his shield at the ready.'

He nodded. 'And when you do that, there are always some people who only see the shield.'

'Yes, you know about that, don't you?' She gave a wry smile. 'We're not so different, you and I. Your defence is glaring at people, mine is laughter and pretending never to mind about anything.'

'I had begun to understand that,' he said. 'But I didn't really see behind it until now. Your shield is more skilful than mine.'

'Nobody sees behind it unless I show them. But I can show you because of what you give me.'

'I need you more than any man has ever needed a woman since the dawn of time,' he said slowly.

'You need me as nobody else ever has or ever will, and that's the greatest gift in the world. Nobody has ever given it to me before, and I don't want it from anyone else. You've made me complete. I was afraid I'd go through life without ever having that feeling.'

He laid his forehead against her.

'And I was afraid you'd find me too demanding,' he said.

'You could never be demanding enough,' she assured him. 'The more you demand, the more you fulfil me. You've given me life, as though my real self had only just been born. I don't think you really understand that yet, but you will, my love. It will take time.'

'And we have all the time in the world,' he said, taking her into his arms.

Now their lovemaking was different, infused with the knowledge of each other's heart that they had just discovered. To Petra it was more like a wedding night than the real one she'd known years ago.

At some time in the dawn he murmured, 'There's a story of how, after Achilles' death, he was honoured as a great lord among the other dead souls. But he longed only to be alive and said he would rather return to live on earth as a servant than stay among the dead as a lord. I never understood that story until now.'

'You mean,' she mused, 'that if I were to treat you like a servant, that would be fine as long as you were with me?'

He considered. 'Can I think about that some more?'

He felt her shaking against him and joined in her laughter. She watched him with delight and saw an answering delight in his eyes. He touched her face and spoke softly.

'Love me,' he said in a voice that almost pleaded. 'Love me.'

She knew a surge of joy and reached out to caress him, draw him back into her arms and show him that he belonged there. They made love slowly, yet with a subtle intensity that said more than a million words.

It was much later that it occurred to her that he'd said not, *Make love to me*, but 'Love me.' And only when it was too late did she understand the distinction.

Next day he swept her out into the car and drove down to the shore.

'But not the same as last time,' he said. 'This is a fishing village—at least it was when this island still had a thriving fishing industry. Now they cater for tourists who are interested in fishing. It's time you met my friends.'

His friends turned out to be a family of one-time fishermen, who greeted Lysandros like a long-lost brother and drew Petra into the warmth.

There seemed to be dozens of them. She lost track of the husbands, wives, sons, daughters, cousins, nieces and nephews. She only knew that they all smiled and treated Lysandros as one of the family.

'My mother brought me here for a holiday when I was a kid,' he explained. 'I ran off to go exploring, got lost and the family rescued me. We've been the best of friends ever since.'

She guessed that they'd been well rewarded. The fishing boat on which they now ran tourist expeditions was top of the range. But it was hard to be cynical about these people and when Kyros, the patriarch, said that the nicest thing about Lysandros was not his generosity but the days when he could find time to visit she felt inclined to believe it.

He seemed to size her up, finally deciding that he could trust her with further confidences.

'One day, years ago,' he told her, 'we found him wandering alone on the beach. We hadn't known that he was coming here. He hadn't let us know, or come to the house. Later he said he'd meant to visit us but he arrived in the early morning when the beach was deserted and he thought he'd take a walk. He walked there for hours. A friend saw him and told us. I went down there and walked with him for a while, but he wouldn't come home with me.

'Then my sons took over and they walked with him all night, up and down, up and down, the length of the beach. He was like a machine, talking only in grunts. At last he began to slow down and we managed to persuade him to come with us. We put him to bed and he slept for two days.'

'Did he ever tell you what made him like that?' Petra asked.

'I don't think he knew a lot about it. He just seemed to have been lost in another world, one he couldn't remember or didn't want to remember. We didn't press him. He was our friend, in trouble, and that's all we needed to know. We did suggest that he should see a doctor, but he said we had been his doctors and he wanted no other. I've never seen him like that again so perhaps we were able to make him a little better. I hope so, anyway. He's such a nice guy.'

It was obvious that he knew nothing of the reality of Lysandros's life. The well-known name Demetriou told him that this was a businessman, rich enough to buy them the boat, but they had no conception of the full extent of his fortune and power.

And that was why they mattered to him so much, Petra realised. They were the close-knit, loving, knockabout family he'd never had and would have loved to have. To them he was 'a nice guy', a little removed by his money, but not enough to stop him being one of them.

Unlike virtually everyone else, they neither feared him nor

showed exaggerated respect, which was a relief to him. Instead, they ribbed him mercilessly, yelled cheerful insults, challenged him to races along the sand and rioted when they beat him.

The girls cast soulful eyes at his handsome face and powerful, elegant movements, but their husbands and boyfriends pulled them firmly aside, glaring possessively, daring Lysandros to try to take advantage, forgiving when he didn't.

How different from the Athens husbands who would pimp their wives into his bed in exchange for a contract. No wonder Lysandros loved coming here. It was his only contact with normal life, and the sight of him relishing it was as much a revelation as anything she'd learned in the last few days. He even helped Kyros's wife, Eudora, with the cooking.

Later Eudora whispered in her ear, 'You're the only woman he's ever brought here. That's why everyone's looking at you. Don't tell him I told you.'

She gave a satisfied nod, as though she personally had brought about the miracle, and scurried away.

Afterwards they went out in the boat. Dressed in a swimsuit, Petra sat in the prow, wondering if life could get any better than this.

She drew a deep contented breath, looking up at the sky, then around her at the sea and the horizon. There, a little distance away in the boat, were Lysandros and Kyros chatting casually, laughing in the easy way of friends.

Then she blinked, uncertain whether she'd seen what she thought she'd seen.

Was she going mad, or had Kyros cocked his head significantly in her direction, mouthing the words, 'Is she—the one?'

And had Lysandros nodded?

I'm fantasising, she told herself hastily. *I can't have read Kyros's lips at this distance. Can I?*

But when she looked again they were both regarding her

with interest. To save her blushes she dived overboard and Lysandros joined her.

'Careful, it's deep out here,' he said, holding out his hands to steady her.

She took them and he trod water, drawing her closer, closer against his bare chest, until he could slip his arms right around her, kissing her while treading water madly. Behind them they could hear cheers and yells from the boat.

When they climbed back on board Kyros hinted slyly that there was a cabin below if they wished. More cheers and yells while his wife told him to behave himself and he silenced her with a kiss. It was that sort of day.

Returning home, they ate their fill before going out into the village square where there was dancing. Lysandros could dance as well as any of them. The girls knew it and queued up for their turn. Petra was untroubled. She had all the male attention she could possibly want, and she was enjoying the sight of him unselfconscious and actually seeming happy.

He saw her watching him and waved before being drawn back into the dance by three young females at once, while their menfolk looked on wryly. At the end he blew each of them a kiss before holding out his hands to Petra and drawing her onto the floor.

'Dance with me,' he murmured. 'And save me from getting my throat cut.'

He was showing her off in public, but why? To make a point to the others, or simply because he was more than a little tipsy? Joyfully she decided that she didn't care. This was the man nature had meant him to be before the demons got their destructive hands on him, and if it was the last thing she did she would open the door that led back to that world and lead him through it.

'We ought to be going,' he gasped at last. 'The trouble is, that wine Kyros serves is…well…' He sat down suddenly.

'And everyone else is as woozy as you,' she said. 'Even me.'

'I'm not.' The young man who spoke was the eldest son of the house, wore a priest's garb and was stone cold sober. 'I'll drive you home.'

'And I'll pay for your taxi back,' Lysandros said sleepily. 'Done.'

On the way home they sat in the back, with his head on her shoulder, his eyes closed. As the car came to a halt the priest looked back and grinned.

'I've never seen him let go like that before,' he said. 'I congratulate you.'

She didn't ask what he meant. She didn't need to. Her spirits were soaring.

Lysandros awoke long enough to hand over a bundle of notes. 'That'll pay for the taxi. Anything over, put it in the collection box.'

The priest's eyes popped as he saw the amount.

'But do you know how much you've given—?'

'Goodnight!' Lysandros was halfway up the path.

She undressed him while he lay back and let her do all the work.

'You think you're a sultan being attended by the harem,' she observed as she finished.

He opened one eye. 'It seemed only fair to show you that I can behave as badly as any other man who dances with a dozen women, gets smashed out of his mind and lets his wife wait on him. Goodnight.'

He rolled over and went to sleep on his front, leaving her with the view of the most perfectly shaped male behind she'd ever seen, and wondering if he knew he'd called her his wife.

He slept late next morning, unusual for him. She rose and

made coffee, returning to find him leaning back against the pillow, one arm behind his head and a wicked look in his eyes. Nor was the wickedness confined to his eyes. A glance at the rest of him told her that he was ready to make up for the deficiencies of the night before.

But she decided not to indulge him at once. They drank coffee sedately, although the look in his eyes was far from sedate. She showed no sign of noticing this, but after a while she slipped off her flimsy silk nightdress and began to find small jobs to do about the room, knowing that they gave him a perfect view of her from various angles.

'Do you have to do that?' he asked in a strained voice.

'Well, I thought one of us should do some tidying up,' she said innocently.

'Come here!'

Wasting no further time, she raced to the bed and took him in her arms.

'Just let me love you,' she said.

'As long as you do love me,' he said heavily.

'I do. I always will.'

He would have spoken again but she silenced him by laying her mouth against his, taking his attention so that at first he didn't notice her softly wandering hands until the excitement building with her caresses overtook him totally and he drew a long shuddering breath.

'I have ruthless ways of making my wishes known,' she whispered against his mouth.

'I believe you,' he groaned.

'You think you know me, but you haven't begun to discover what I'm capable of.'

'Why don't you—show me?'

She let her fingers explore a little further, reaching the

place between his legs where his response was rapidly growing out of control. 'Like that?'

'Just like that.'

Now her fingers were enclosing their object, revelling in its size and the thought of having it inside her. Then she moved over him so that she could fit her legs astride him and make him hers in her own way.

She had the glorious sense of being able to do anything she wanted. Everything was right because they were together and did everything together. It was right to celebrate their hearts but also right to celebrate their bodies as they were doing now. So she did as she pleased, confident of pleasing him at the same time, and knew by his expression that she'd outdone herself.

'That was very nice,' she said, luxuriating in his arms afterwards.

'Very nice?' he growled. 'Is that the best you can say?'

'Do you have anything else to suggest?'

'Oh, yes,' he said. 'I have plenty more to suggest. Come here—'

'Suppose I don't want to?'

'You've left it much too late to say that. *Now, come here.*'

Carolling with laughter, she raised her arms over her head and cried, 'Shan't!'

'Oh, yes, you will.'

So she did.

When Lysandros's cellphone began to ring he regarded it for a long time before saying reluctantly, 'I suppose I ought to answer that.'

'I'm amazed you haven't been on the phone more often,' she said. 'In fact I'm amazed it hasn't rung more often.'

'I gave strict instructions to my staff not to disturb me unless it was vital. Linos, my assistant, is pretty good that way.

He's called a couple of times, I've given him instructions for managing without me and so far he's not done too badly. But I suppose—' He sighed.

'We have to get back to the real world.'

He kissed her. 'After this, the real world will be different.' He answered the phone. 'Yes, Linos? Oh, no, what's happened? All right, all right, one thing at a time.'

Sad but resigned, Petra made her way upstairs to start packing. The dream life couldn't last for ever, and now was the time to see if it could be carried into reality. The omens were good.

'I've called the airport,' she said when Lysandros appeared. 'There's a flight to Athens in a couple of hours.'

He sighed and put his arms around her. 'I wish you'd said a couple of years, but I suppose we have to take it. There's a big meeting coming up that Linos says he can't manage without me.'

'It had to happen some time,' she said. 'The sound of battle, summoning you to the fray.'

'It's funny how that doesn't sound so good any more. But you'll be with me, and we can start making plans.'

Her lips twitched. 'Plans for what?'

He rested his forehead against hers. 'Plans for the future, and if I have to explain that to you, then I've been wasting my time recently. Unfortunately, this isn't the moment to make the point. But I think you know what I'm talking about.'

Marriage. He hadn't posed a formal question but he acted as though matters were already settled between them, and she knew it was a sign of their closeness that he felt free to do so.

She went with him upstairs to take a last look at the smashed room he'd shared with Brigitta, but she refused to go with him to the grave.

'You need to say goodbye to her alone,' she said gently. 'If I'm there it will spoil it for her.'

'How can you speak so?' he asked in wonder. 'As though she was real to you, as if you'd met her and talked to her.'

'They say that nobody ever comes back across the River Styx,' she mused, speaking of the river that ran between earth and Hades, as the underworld was often known. 'But I wonder. If someone has something important enough, a message that they simply must deliver—well, let's just say that I think some part of her might still be there. But she wants you to talk to her alone. I don't really belong here.'

He frowned. 'Do you mean not to come back to this house with me?'

'I don't think she wants me to. This is her place. You and I can have somewhere else. Keep this for her, to honour her.'

Her words fell like blessed balm on his soul. He'd been wondering how to solve this conundrum, fearing that the part of his heart that remained loyal to the past might offend her. But she'd understood, as she understood everything about him. He kissed her and walked out into the grounds, offering thanks as he went.

Petra watched him until he disappeared.

The grave lay quiet in the afternoon sun, with only the faintest breeze disturbing the branches of the trees overhead. Lysandros stood there for a long time, listening, but there was only silence.

'Perhaps she imagined it,' he whispered at last, 'or perhaps you really can talk to her and not to me. We never could open our hearts to each other, could we?'

Overhead, the leaves rustled.

'I tried my best. Do you remember how desperately I talked to you as you prepared to cross the eternal river with our child in your arms? But you never looked back, and I knew I'd failed you yet again. That failure will be with me always.

'Petra was right to say that I honour you still, and that will last for ever. This place will always be yours and no other woman's. Nothing can change that.

'But there has been a change in me—can you forgive that, if nothing else? It seems almost wrong to find happiness with her after so much that we could have had, and lost, but I can't help myself. She is everything to me, yet I still—*honour* you.'

He couldn't have said what he was hoping for, but nothing came—no sign, no message, no absolution. Only the wind became stronger until it was gusting fiercely in the trees, shaking the branches. Autumn was still some way off, yet the leaves were falling, seeming to bring the darkness closer.

Suddenly he couldn't bear to stay here. Turning, he hurried back to the light.

At the Villa Lukas the air was buzzing with the news that the bride and groom would soon be home from their honeymoon.

'Such a party there's going to be!' Aminta carolled. '*Everyone* is coming—the press, the television cameras—'

'Any guests?' teased Petra.

'All the most important people,' Aminta said blissfully.

'No, I mean real guests—friends, people the host would want anyway, even if the press have never heard of them.'

Aminta stared at her, baffled. It was clear that after years of working for a billionaire shipping magnate she barely understood the concept of friendship for its own sake, so Petra laughed and went on her way. After all this time as part of a film star's retinue, why was she surprised? Perhaps because her time alone with Lysandros had caused a seismic shift in her perceptions.

As soon as she reached her bedroom there was a call from Estelle, full of excitement at the rumours.

'You and Lysandros were seen together on Corfu, going out in a boat and driving through the streets. Come on, tell!'

'There's nothing to tell,' Petra said primly.

'Hmm! As good as that, eh? We'll invite him to our party and take a good look at you two together.'

'I shall warn him not to come.'

'You won't, you know.' Chuckling, she hung up.

The next call was from Lysandros to say he had to return to Piraeus. 'So it'll be several days before we see each other,' he said with a sigh.

'Just be back for the big party next week. Then it's all going to descend on us.'

He laughed. 'I promise to be there. I don't know how I'm going to manage being away from you.'

'Just come back to me,' she said tenderly.

When the call was over she sat smiling. Looking up, she caught a glimpse of herself in the mirror and laughed.

'I look like an idiot. I feel like an idiot. So I guess that makes me an idiot. I don't care. I didn't know there was this much happiness on earth.'

From the corridor outside came the sound of footsteps. Then the door was flung open and Nikator stood on the threshold. His eyes were bright, his face flushed, his chest heaving, and Petra knew there was going to be trouble.

'Hello, brother, dear,' she said brightly, slightly emphasising 'brother'. But it was useless and she knew it.

'Don't say that,' Nikator hurled at her. 'Oh, Petra, don't say that!'

He dropped to his knees beside her, reaching out to clasp her around the waist, and she had to fight not to recoil. Their last meeting had been two weeks ago, just before she'd gone to Corfu. Nikator had implored her to stay, upset when she refused, desperate when she wouldn't tell him where she was going.

The same exaggerated look was on his face now, making her say soothingly, 'You don't want me to call you "dear"?

All right, I won't, especially as I'm angry with you. How dare
you let Lysandros think we'd gone to England together?'

He reached up to seize her in a fumbling grip. She tried to
free herself but found there was unexpected steel behind the
childish movements.

'I couldn't help it. I love you so much I'm not responsible
for my actions. I wanted to save you from Demetriou—'

'But I didn't want to be saved,' she said, trying to introduce
a note of common sense. 'I love him. Try to understand that.
I love *him*, not you.'

'That's because you don't know what he's like. You think
you do. You believe what he told you about Brigitta, but there
was no need for her to die. If he hadn't bullied her mercilessly
she wouldn't have been alone when—'

He pulled himself up far enough to sit on the bed beside
her, his hands gripping her shoulders.

'He's fooled you,' he gasped. 'He only wants you because
you're mine. He has to take everything that's mine. It's been
that way all my life.'

'Nikki—'

'You don't know what it's been like, always being told that
the Demetriou family were lucky because they had a worthy
son to take over, but my father only had me. Everyone admires
him because he brutalises people into submission. But not me.
I can't be brutal.'

'But you can be sneaky, can't you? Grow up, little boy!'

'Don't call me that,' he screamed. 'I'm not a child; I'll show
you.'

She tried to push him off but his grip tightened. He rose to
his feet, thrusting her back against the bed and hurling himself
on top of her. Next thing, his mouth was over hers and he was
trying to thrust his tongue between her lips.

Frantically she twisted her head away, trying to put up a hand to protect her mouth and writhing this way and that to avoid him.

'Get off me,' she gasped. 'Nikki, do you hear? *Get off me!*'

'Don't fight me. Let me love you—let me save you—'

With a last heave she managed to get out from under him, shoving him so hard that he fell to the floor. In a flash she was on her feet, dashing to the door, yanking it open.

'Clear out and don't come back!' she snapped.

But he made another lunge, forcing her to take drastic action with her knee. A yowl broke from him and he clutched himself between the legs, stumbling out into the corridor under the interested eyes of several maids.

He got to his feet, his eyes burning.

'You'll regret that,' he said softly.

'Not half as much as you'll regret it if you bother me again,' she snapped.

He threw a look of pure hatred at the servants and hurried away.

'Thanks, miss,' one of the maids said.

From which Petra deduced that several of them had been longing to do the very same thing.

Returning to her room, she tried to calm down. She'd known Nikator could be unpleasant but he was worse than she'd imagined.

In her agitation she forgot to wonder how he knew that Lysandros had told her about Brigitta.

CHAPTER ELEVEN

Two days later Homer and Estelle made a grand and glorious return, under the gaze of carefully arranged cameras. Plans for the party started at once, although first Aminta had a servant problem to deal with. Nikator had made certain accusations against the maids, who pleaded with Petra for help, which she gave.

'I'm sorry, Homer, I don't want to quarrel with you or your son,' she said, 'but Nikator was limping when he left and I'm afraid the maids saw. So now he has a grudge against them.'

Homer was a wise man and he knew his son's bad side. He believed her, thanked her, told Nikator to stop talking nonsense and made him apologise to Petra. Instead of the explosion of temper she'd feared, Nikator seemed to be in a chastened mood.

'Which means he's more dangerous than ever,' Lysandros said as they dined together. 'The sooner you're out of there the better. In the meantime I'll have a quiet word with him.'

'No, don't,' she begged. 'I'm quite capable of having my own quiet word, as he's already discovered. I'm only afraid he'll spin you some silly story about him and me—'

'Which you think I'll be stupid enough to believe?' Lysandros queried wryly. 'Credit me with more intelligence than that.'

Nikator seemed to be making an effort. She went downstairs once to find him with a large painting that he'd bought as a gift for his father. It depicted the Furies, terrifying creatures with snakes for hair and blood dripping from their eyes. Petra studied the picture with interest. She'd been conscious of the Furies recently, but now she felt free from them.

'The point was, they never let up,' Nikator said. 'Once they started on you, they'd hound you for ever.'

She wondered if he was sending a message that he would never forgive her for offending him. He would harm her or Lysandros if he could, she was sure of it. But they were both on the watch for him, and surely there was nothing in his power.

The party was going to be the society event of the season. Fellow film stars from Hollywood were flying in to dance, sing and raise their glasses in the fake Parthenon. Every businessman in Athens would be there, hoping to meet a film star, plus some film makers hoping to secure backing from rich men.

When the night came there was no sign of Nikator. Homer grumbled about the disrespect to his bride, but Petra also thought she detected a note of relief.

'Maybe when you and Lysandros are formally engaged it might be easier,' her mother said quietly. 'He'll have to accept it then. Just don't take too long about it. It might be the best thing for everyone.'

'But surely Lysandros is the foe?'

'A rival, not a foe. If the two families could come together Homer thinks it might be wonderful.'

'What about Nikator? Surely Homer wouldn't cut his son out?'

'Not out of his life or his heart, but out of the shipping business, yes. He could buy him a gaming house, or something else that would give him a good life without threatening people's jobs in the shipyard.'

It seemed the perfect solution, but Petra wondered if it would offend Nikator's pride and increase his hatred of Lysandros. Mentally she put it aside to be worried about later. For now all she cared about was the coming evening, when she would see her lover again and dance in his arms.

She'd chosen a dress of blue satin, so dark that it was almost black. It was a tight fit, emphasising her perfect shape, but with a modest neckline, to please Lysandros.

How handsome he was, she thought, watching him approach. Homer greeted him enthusiastically; he replied with smiles and expressions of civility. Petra remembered how Lysandros had cleared Homer of any involvement in Brigitta's tragedy, saying, 'To do him justice, he's a fairly decent man, a lot better than many in this business.'

So it was true what Estelle had suggested. Her marriage to Lysandros might signal a new dawn in the Greek shipping business, and everyone knew it. Including Nikator.

Lysandros did the usual networking with Petra on his arm, and everyone had the chance to study them as a couple.

'Has anyone told you what they're all thinking?' he murmured as they danced.

'They were lining up to tell me,' she said with a laugh. 'We were watched in Corfu. Estelle says we were seen together, driving through the streets and on the boat.'

He shrugged. 'They're public places. People were bound to see us. When we marry, I suppose that will be in public as well—' He smiled and added softly, 'At least, the first part of it will.'

'Oh, really?' she murmured. 'I don't remember getting a proposal.'

'You've had a proposal every minute of the last few days and you know it,' he said firmly. He rather spoilt the autocratic sound of this by murmuring, 'Siren,' so softly that his breath on her cheek was almost all she knew.

'Don't I get an answer?' he asked.

'You had your answer the first time we made love,' she said. 'And you hadn't even asked me.'

'But now I've asked and you've answered, we might tell them,' he suggested.

'Tell this crowd? I thought you'd hate to be stared at.'

'As long as they see what I want them to see, that's all right. If they watch me walking off with the most beautiful woman in the room, I can live with that.'

He tightened his arm around her waist, swirling her around and around while everyone laughed and applauded. Petra remembered that later because it was almost her last moment of unclouded joy.

As they came out of the swirl and her head began to clear she saw something that made her sigh. Even so, she didn't realise that disaster had walked in. Disaster was called Nikator, and he had a smile on his face. It was a cold, tense smile, but even so it gave no sign of what was about to crash down on her.

'What's he up to?' she asked as he embraced Homer and Estelle.

'Trying to win forgiveness for turning up late,' Lysandros remarked. 'Pretend he doesn't exist, as I'm doing.'

His words reminded her of how hard it must be for him to appear at ease in Nikator's presence, and she smiled at him in reassurance.

'Better still,' Lysandros said, 'let's show him exactly where he stands.'

Before she knew what he meant to do, he'd pulled her closer and laid his mouth on hers in a long kiss, whose meaning left nothing to the imagination.

Now he'd made his declaration to the world. This man, who'd spent so long hiding his true self behind protective bolts and bars, had finally managed to throw them aside and break out to freedom because the one special woman had given him the key. He no longer cared who could look into his soul because her love had made him invincible.

As the kiss ended and he raised his head, his manner was that of a victor. A hero, driving his chariot across the battlefield where his enemies lay defeated, might have worn that air of triumph.

'Let him do what he likes,' he murmured to her. 'Nothing can touch us now.'

She was to remember those words long after.

'Ah!' cried Nikator. 'Isn't love charming?'

His caustic voice shattered her dream and made her shudder. Nikator had marched across the floor and stood regarding them sardonically, while Homer hurried behind and laid an urgent hand on his son's arm. Nikator threw it off.

'Leave me, Father; there are things that have to be said and I'm going to enjoy saying them.' He grinned straight at Lysandros. 'I never thought the day would come when I'd have a good laugh at you. You, of all men, to be taken in by a designing woman!'

'Give up,' Lysandros advised him gently. 'It's no use, Nikator.'

'But that's what's so funny,' Nikator yelped. 'How easily you were fooled when you fancied yourself so armoured. *But the armour doesn't cover the heel, does it?*'

Even this jibe didn't seem to affect Lysandros, who continued to regard Nikator with pity and contempt.

'And your "heel" was that you believed in her,' Nikator said, jabbing a finger at Petra. 'You're too stupid to realise that she's been playing you for a sucker because there's something she wanted.'

'Hey, you!' Estelle thumped him hard on the shoulder. 'If you're suggesting my daughter has to marry for money, let me tell you—'

'Not money!' Nikator spat. 'Glory. Anything for a good story, eh?'

'What the hell are you talking about?' Lysandros demanded. 'There's no story.'

'Of course there is. It's what she lives by, her reputation, getting a new angle on things that nobody else can get. And, oh, boy, did she get it this time!'

Even then they didn't see the danger. Lysandros sighed, shaking his head as if being patient with a tiresome infant.

'You won't laugh when you know what she's been doing,' Nikator jeered. 'Getting onto the press, telling them your secrets, repeating what you said to her—'

'That's a lie!' Petra cried.

'Of course it's a lie,' Lysandros said.

The smiling confidence had vanished from his face and his voice had the deadly quiet of a man who was fighting shock, but he was still uttering the right words.

'Be careful what you say,' he told Nikator coldly. 'I won't have her slandered.'

'Oh, you think it's a slander, do you? Then how does the press know what you said to her at the Achilleion? How do they know you showed her Brigitta's grave and told her how often you'd stood there and begged Brigitta's forgiveness? Have you ever repeated that? No, I thought not. But someone has.'

'Not me,' Petra said, aghast. 'I would never—you can't believe that!'

She flung the last words at Lysandros, who turned and said quickly, 'Of course not.'

But his manner was strained. Gone was the relaxed joy of only a few minutes ago. Only two of them knew what he had said to her at that grave.

'It's about time you saw this,' Nikator said.

Nobody had noticed the bag he'd brought with him and dropped at his feet. Now he leaned down and began to pull out the contents, distributing them to the fascinated crowd.

They were newspapers, carrying the banner headline, *The Truth About Achilles: How She Made Him Talk*, and telling the story of the well-known historian Petra Radnor, who'd first come to prominence when, little more than a girl, she'd published *Greek Heroes of the Past*.

The book had been such a success that it had been revised for a school edition and was now being considered for a further revision. This time the angle would be more glamorous and romantic, as Ms Radnor considered Greek men today and whether they really lived up to their classical reputation. For the moment she was working on Achilles.

There followed a detailed description of the last few weeks—their first meeting at the wedding, at which *Ms Radnor exerted all her charms to entice her prey*, the evening they had spent together dancing in the streets, and finally their time on Corfu in the villa where 'Achilles' had once lived with his other lover, who was buried there.

> *Together they visited the Archilleion, where they stood before the great picture of the first Achilles dragging the lifeless body of his enemy behind his chariot, and the modern Achilles explained that he was raised to do it to them before they did it to him.*

Which was exactly what he'd said, Petra thought in numb horror.

It went on and on. Somehow the people behind this had learned every private detail of their time together at the villa, and were parading it for amusement. 'Achilles' had been trapped, deluded, made a fool of by a woman who was always one step ahead of him. That was the message, and those who secretly feared and hated him would love every moment of it.

All around she could see people trying to smother their amusement. Homer was scowling and the older guests feared him too much to laugh aloud, but they were covering their mouths, turning their heads away. The younger ones were less cautious.

'Even you,' Nikator jeered at Lysandros. 'Even you weren't as clever as you reckoned. You thought you had it all sussed, didn't you? But she saw through you, and oh, what a story she's going to get out of it, *Achilles!*'

Lysandros didn't move. He seemed to have been turned to stone.

Nikator swung his attention around to Petra.

'Not that you've been so clever yourself, *my dear deluded sister.*'

Estelle gave a little shriek and Homer grabbed his son.

'That's enough,' he snapped. 'Leave here at once.'

But Nikator threw him off again. Possessed by bitter fury, he could defy even his father. He went closer to Petra, almost hissing in her face.

'He's a fool if he believed you, but you're a fool if you believed him. There are a hundred women in this room right now who trusted him and discovered their mistake too late. You're just another.'

Somehow she forced herself to speak.

'No, Nikator, that's not true. I know you want to believe it, but it's not true.'

'You're deluded,' he said contemptuously.

'No, it's you who are deluded,' she retorted at once.

'Have you no eyes?'

'Yes, I have eyes, but eyes can deceive you. What matters

isn't what your eyes tell you, but what your heart tells you. And my heart says that this is the man I trust with all of me.' She lifted her head and spoke loudly. 'Whatever Lysandros tells me, that is the truth.'

She stepped close to him and took his hand. It was cold as ice.

'Let's go, my dearest,' she said. 'We don't belong here.'

The crowd parted for them as they walked away together into the starry night. Now the onlookers were almost silent, but it was a terrible silence, full of horror and derision.

On and on they walked, into the dark part of the grounds. Here there were only a few stragglers and they fell away when they saw them coming, awed, or perhaps made fearful, by the sight of two faces that seemed to be looking into a different world.

At last they came to a small wooden bridge over a river and went to stand in the centre, gazing out over the water. Still he didn't look at her, but at last he spoke in a low, almost despairing voice.

'Thank you for what you said about always believing me.'

'It was only what you said to me first,' she said fervently. 'I was glad to return it. I meant it every bit as much as you did. Nikator is lying. Yes, there was a book, years ago, but I told you about that myself, and about the reissue.'

'And the new version?'

'I knew they were thinking of bringing it out again, but not in detail. And it certainly isn't going to be anything like Nikator said. Lysandros, you can't believe all that stuff about my "working on Achilles" and pursuing you to make use of you. It isn't true. I swear it isn't.'

'Of course it isn't,' he said quietly. 'But—'

The silence was almost tangible, full of jagged pain.

'But what?' she asked, not daring to believe the suspicions rioting in her brain.

'How did they discover what we said?' he asked in a rasping, tortured voice. 'That's all I want to know.'

'And I can't tell you because I don't know. It wasn't me. Maybe someone was standing behind us at the Achilleion—'

'Someone who knew who we were? And the grave? How do they know about that?'

'I don't know,' she whispered. 'I don't know. I never repeated anything to anybody. *Lysandros, you have got to believe me.*'

She looked up into his face and spoke with all the passion at her command.

'Can't you see that we've come to the crossroads? This is it. This is where we find out if it all meant anything. I am telling you the truth. Nobody in the world matters more to me than you, and I would never, ever lie to you. For pity's sake, say that you believe me, *please.*'

The terrible silence was a thousand fathoms deep. Then he stammered, 'Of course…I do believe you…' But there was agony in his voice and she could hear the effort he put into forcing himself.

'*You don't,*' she said explosively as the shattering truth hit her. 'All that about trusting me—it was just words.'

'No, I—*no!*'

'*Yes!*'

'I tried to mean them, I wanted to, but—'

Her heart almost failed her, for there on his face was the look she'd seen before, on the statue at the Achilleion, when Achilles tried to draw the arrow from his foot, his expression full of despair as he realised there was no way to escape his fate.

'Yes—*but,*' she said bitterly. 'I should have known there'd be a "but".'

'Nobody else knows about that grave,' he said hoarsely. 'I can't get past that.'

'Perhaps Nikator does know. Perhaps he had someone following us—'

'That wouldn't help them find the grave. It's deep in the grounds; you can't see it from outside. I've never told anyone else. You're the one person I've ever trusted enough to…to…'

As the words died he groaned and reached for her. It would have been simple to go into his arms and try to rediscover each other that way, but a spurt of anger made her step back, staring at him with hard eyes.

'And that's the worst thing you can do to anyone,' she said emphatically. 'The more you trust someone, the worse it is when they betray you.'

He stared at her like a man lost in a mist, vainly trying to understand distant echoes. 'What did you say?' he whispered.

'Don't you recognise your own words, Lysandros? Words you said to me in Las Vegas. I'll remind you of some more. "Nobody is ever as good as you think they are, and sooner or later the truth is always there. Better to have no illusions, and be strong." You really meant that, didn't you? I didn't realise until now just how much you meant it.'

'Don't remind me of that time,' he shouted. 'It's over.'

'It'll never be over because you carry it with you, and all the hatred and suspicion that was in you then is there still. You just hide it better, but then something happens and it speaks, telling you to play safe and think the worst of everyone. Even me. Look into your heart and be honest. Suddenly I look just like all the others, don't I? Lying, scheming—'

'Shut up!' he roared. 'Don't talk like that. I forbid it.'

'Why, because it comes too close to the truth? And who are you to forbid me?'

If his mind had been clearer he could have told her that he was the man whose fate she held in her hands, but the clearheadedness for which he was famed seemed to have deserted him now and everything was in a whirl of confusion.

'I *want* to believe you; can't you understand that?' He gripped her shoulders tightly, almost shaking her. 'But tell me how. Show me a way. *Tell me!'*

His misery was desperate. If her own heart hadn't been breaking, she would have been filled with pity for him.

'I can't tell you,' she said. 'That's one thing you must find for yourself.'

'Petra—please—try to understand—'

'But I do. I only wish I didn't. I understand that nothing has changed. We thought things could be different now. I love you and I hoped you loved me—'

'But I do, you know that—'

'No, even *you* don't know that. The barriers are still there, shutting you off from the world, from me. I thought I could break them down, but I can't.'

'If you can't, nobody can,' he said despairingly. Then something seemed to happen to him. His hands fell, he stepped back, and when he spoke again it was with the calm of despair. 'And perhaps that's all there is to be said.'

There was a noise from the distance, lights; the party was breaking up. People streamed out into the garden and now the laughter could be clearly heard, rising on the night air.

And the derision would torture him as well as the loss of his faith in her. Bleakly she wondered which one troubled him more.

'I'll be in touch,' he told her. 'There are ways of getting to the bottom of this.'

'Of course,' she said formally, waiting for his kiss.

Briefly he rested his fingertips against her cheek, but apart from that he departed without touching her.

* * *

The detective work was relatively easy. It didn't take long to establish that the 'newspaper copies' were forgeries, specially printed at Nikator's orders, the text written to Nikator's dictation.

But that helped little. It was the overheard conversations that were really damaging, the fact that they couldn't be explained, and the fact that hundreds of people at the party had read them.

Calling her publishers, Petra told them to abandon plans for a reissue of her book. They were dismayed.

'But we've heard such exciting stories—'

'None of them are true,' she snapped. 'Forget it.'

She and Lysandros were still in touch, but only just. They exchanged polite text messages, and she understood. He was avoiding her and she knew why. If they had met face to face he wouldn't have known what to say to her. He was back stranded again in the sea of desolation, unable to reach out to the one person who'd helped him in the past.

Or perhaps he just didn't know how to tell her that the break was coming and there was no escape.

It might have been different, she knew. By quarrelling, they had done exactly what Nikator had wanted.

But it went deeper than that. However it looked, Nikator hadn't really caused the chasm between them; he'd merely revealed its existence. Sooner or later the crack in their relationship would have come to light.

Sometimes she blamed herself for the anger that had made her attack him when he was wretched, but in her heart she knew it changed nothing. He was the man he was, and the hope she'd briefly glimpsed was no more than an illusion.

In her present bitter mood she wondered how much of her view of him had been real, and how much she'd shaped him to fit her own desires. Had he really needed her so much, or had she just refused to see that he was self-contained, needing neither her nor anyone else? It was suddenly easy to believe that, and to feel alone and unwanted as never before in her life.

'Surplus to requirements,' she thought angrily as she lay in bed one night. 'A silly woman who reshaped her image of a man to suit herself. And got her just deserts.'

In a fury of despair and frustration, she began to bang her head on the pillow and only stopped when she realised that she was mirroring his movements. She wished he were there so that she could share it with him.

But would he ever be with her again?

In Homer's library she found her own volume, the one on which Nikator had built his attacks.

'Now I know where he got the idea,' she thought wryly, turning to the Achilles section and reading her own text.

His name had been linked with many women, but the one for whose love he'd given his life was Polyxena, daughter of King Priam of Troy. His love for her had held out the hope of a peace treaty between the Greeks and the Trojans, and an end to the war. But Paris was enraged. Such a treaty would have meant he had to return Helen to her husband, and that he was determined not to do.

Through his spies he knew that Achilles could only be destroyed through his heel and he haunted the temple, waiting for the wedding. When Achilles appeared Paris shot him in the heel with a poisoned arrow.

In a further twist to the tale, Achilles' ghost was reputed to have spoken from the grave, demanding that Polyxena be sacrificed and forced to join him in death. Whereupon she was dragged to the altar and slain.

And what happened after that? Petra wondered. Had he met

her in a boat on the River Styx, ready to convey her to the underworld? Had she told him that he couldn't really have loved her or he would have behaved more generously? Or had he accused her of betraying him, giving that as his reason for condemning her to death? One way or another, it had ended badly, as many love affairs did.

Or was the story wrong? Had he not forced her to join him in death, but merely implored her, knowing that she would be glad to join him? When they met at the Styx had he held out his arms to her, and had she run to him?

I'm going crazy, she thought. I've got to stop thinking like this.

Stop thinking about him. That was all it would take.

It would never happen unless they could find some point of closure. And she could think of nothing that would provide a definite answer.

Unless…

Slowly she straightened up in her seat, staring into the distance, seeing nothing but the inspiration that had come to her.

That's what it needs, she thought. Of course! *Why didn't I think of that before?*

CHAPTER TWELVE

THE text message was simple and heartfelt.

I need to talk to you. Why have you stopped replying? L

He hesitated before sending it, afflicted by a feeling that the world had turned on its head. He'd received so many texts like this, but never before had he sent one. Would she reply to him as he had so often replied to the others? The thought sent him cold with alarm. But he must do this. He could no longer endure the silence between them. He pressed the button.

Her reply was quick.

I'm sorry. I needed to be alone to think. P

He answered, *I thought that, but it's a mistake. We must do our thinking together. L*

She texted back, *We only hurt each other.*

This time he sent her only one word. *Please.*

She called back and he heard her voice.

'Please, Lysandros, it's better if we don't talk for a while.'

'No,' he said stubbornly. 'It isn't. There's a way out of this—'

'Not if you don't believe me. And in your heart you don't. Goodbye—my dearest.'

As she hung up he passed a hand over his eyes, troubled

by something he'd heard in the background, something he couldn't quite place—something—

He bounded to his feet, swearing. A tannoy announcement. That was what he'd heard. She was at the airport.

Frantically he called back, but she'd switched off. Neither speech nor text could reach her now. She was on her way back to England.

The world was coming down about his ears. Once she was gone he'd lose her for ever; he knew that well. And then everything would end.

He moved like lightning, calling his private pilot. A moment later he was rushing through the grounds to the landing stage where his helicopter waited, and a few minutes after that they were in the air.

While the pilot radioed ahead to the airport, arranging for a landing and a car to meet them, he called Information to check the next flight to England. It would take off in half an hour. He groaned.

The pilot was skilful and made Athens Airport in the fastest possible time. The car was waiting, taking him to the main building. As he stared out of the window he prayed for a delay, something that would give him the chance to get her off the plane. But then he saw it, rising into the sky, higher and higher, taking his life with it.

Even so, he clung to hope until the last minute. Only the word *Departed* on the board forced him to accept the brutal truth. She had gone. He'd lost her. His life was over. He almost reeled away from the desk, blinded by misery, wanting to howl up to heaven.

He was pulled up short by a collision. Two arms went around him, supporting him as they had so often done before. He tried to pull himself together.

'I'm sorry, I—*Petra!*'

She was clinging to him, staring up into his face, hardly able to believe what was happening.

'What's the matter?' she asked quickly. 'Why are you here?'

'To stop you leaving. I thought you'd be on that plane for England that just took off. You can't go like this.'

'Like this?' she asked hopefully.

'Not until we've settled things.'

She didn't know what to make of that. It might almost have been business-speak, but he was trembling in her arms.

'I'm not going back to England,' she said. 'That's not why I'm here. Please calm down. You worry me.'

He was taking huge gulps of air as relief shuddered through him.

'Let's find somewhere to sit,' she said, 'and I'll explain.'

Over a drink she said quietly, 'I was going to Corfu. I've been thinking a lot about how Nikator knew what we said, and it seems to me that he must have known a lot more about Priam House than he's ever let anyone know; enough to have bugged the place, even long ago. So I was going to see what I could find.'

'Yes,' he said. 'That's it. We'll find the answer. But why didn't you tell me?'

'I wasn't sure how you'd—well, anyway, I meant to go alone, but when I got here I realised I should tell you first. Because if I find bugs, I need you to be there, don't I? Otherwise—' she gave a wan smile '—otherwise, how will you know I didn't plant them, to clear myself?'

'Don't,' he whispered.

'Anyway, I was just about to leave the airport. I was going to come to you and tell you what I was thinking, but here you are. What brought you here?'

'You. I heard an announcement in the background and I thought you were leaving the country. I had to come and stop you. Look, it doesn't matter about all the other things. I can't let you go.'

'Even though you still doubt me?' she asked wryly. 'No, never mind. We'll worry later. We can't tell how this is going to work out.'

'My helicopter's here. It can take us straight on to Corfu, and we'll find all the answers we need there.'

Petra didn't reply. She knew that everything was far more complicated than he'd understood. They might find some answers, but not all and there were still obstacles to overcome. But this wasn't the time to say so.

For the moment she would enjoy the happiness of seeing him again, even though that happiness was tinged with bitterness and the threat of future misery.

An hour later the helicopter set them down on Corfu. As they covered the last few miles she wondered if this was just a forlorn hope and they were chasing it to avoid facing the truth.

'Does anyone know where Nikator is?' he asked suddenly. 'I've been looking for him, but he seems to have vanished.'

'Nobody's seen him for days.'

'How wise of him to avoid me. It was always the way when he was in trouble,' Lysandros said. 'He never did stick around to face things.'

'You do know that he did this, don't you?'

'I've been finding out. And when we know this last thing—'

Then you'll trust me, she thought. But not until then.

Was she making too much of it? she wondered. He'd come looking for her, desperate to stop her leaving him. Wasn't that enough?

But it wasn't. What still lived in her mind was the look that had fleetingly been on his face when disaster had struck. It had been a look of appalled betrayal, saying that she was no different from all the others. Now something must happen to wipe it out, but she had a terrible fear that nothing ever could.

The house was as they had left it, except that then it had been infused with joy. That had vanished now and its silence was the deadly silence of fear.

Lysandros wasted no time. Gathering tools from the shed, he strode out, through the grounds, under the trees, to the place where Brigitta and her child lay, incongruously at peace. Somehow Brigitta seemed a very real presence now, crying out to Lysandros to remember only her love and forget all else.

In the end he'd managed to do that. But too late.

'Why is he doing this?' Petra asked her spirit. 'Can he really only love and trust me when he has something tangible to hold? Isn't there anything deep inside him that tells him the truth? Those times when our hearts were so close that we were like one, do they count for nothing now?'

She thought she could hear Brigitta's melancholy cry, echoing from Hades, the underworld, across the River Styx and down the centuries. There was no hope in that sound.

'That's it!'

Lysandros's shout broke into her thoughts. He'd been hard at work, digging, scrabbling around the grave. Now there was a look of triumph in his eyes.

'Got them,' he said, holding something up.

'What have you found?' she asked.

'Bugs. Tiny microphones powerful enough to pick up anything, including what we said to each other.'

So she was cleared. She waited for the surge of joy that this should have brought her, but nothing happened.

'So this place was bugged,' she said.

But her heart was still waiting for him to say that he would have believed in her anyway, even if he'd found nothing. Desperately hoping, she nudged him in the right direction.

'But how do you know that I didn't come here earlier and put them there?'

If only he would say, *Because I know you wouldn't do that.*

Instead, beaming and oblivious to the undercurrents, he said, 'Of course you didn't. Look at them, they're old. They've been here for years. Nikator must have had spies that told him about this place and bugged it long ago. He's just been waiting for his moment.'

'Ah, I see. So the evidence clears me.'

'Of course it does.'

He scrambled up out of the grave and seized her shoulders.

'Darling, can't you see how wonderful this is? It makes everything right.'

'Does it?' she whispered.

He barely heard her words and totally missed her meaning.

'Come here,' he said, pulling her to him, kissing her fiercely. 'Now nothing can part us again.'

He seized her hand and began to run back to the house, his face shining with happiness. Upstairs, he kicked in the door of his bedroom and drew her swiftly down on the bed. She had a split second to make up her mind, whether or not to go through with this, for she knew that they were coming to the end. But for that very reason she would allow herself this one last time.

She made love to him as never before, giving him not just her body, but a heart infused with sorrow. Everything in her belonged to him. Soul and spirit were his, and there would never be anyone else. He had spoiled all other men for her, and she would live with that. But she could no longer live with him.

With every tender gesture, every whispered word, she bid him farewell. Each caress was a plea for him to remember always that she had loved him utterly and always would, even though their ways must now lie apart.

They reached their moment together and she saw him smiling down at her in triumph and relief, something that had always been her peak of joy. Afterwards he held her tenderly, protectively, and she had to struggle not to weep.

'Thank goodness,' he said fervently. 'We so nearly lost each other.'

To him it was all so simple. He hadn't faced the inevitable yet, but she must face it for both of them.

'Lysandros—'

'What is it, my darling?'

'Don't you realise that we *have* lost each other?'

'No, how can we? We know how it was all done now. The whole newspaper thing was fake, he had us followed to the Achilleion by someone who eavesdropped on what we said, and now we've found the evidence that clears you.'

As soon as he said the last words he knew what he'd done. She saw it in the sudden dismay that swept over his face.

'Yes,' she said sadly, 'you needed evidence to clear me because my word alone wasn't enough.'

'Don't,' he interrupted her hurriedly. 'Don't say it.'

'I have to. I'm going away—at least for a little while.'

'No. I won't let you go. I'll make you stay until you see sense—' He heard himself and screwed up his eyes in dismay. 'I didn't mean it like that.'

'It's all right. I love it that you want me, but perhaps it isn't right for us. If you only knew how much I've longed for you to believe in me anyway, in the face of all the evidence. Now it's too late.'

'But we've just made everything right.'

'My dearest, we've made nothing right. Can't you see that? We made love, and it was beautiful, but real love is so much more than passion. I know what to do when I'm in your arms. I know the caresses you can't resist, just as you know the ones that affect me. We know how to tempt each other on and on until we explode with desire, and for a while that seems enough. But it soon passes, and then we have to see the distance between us.'

'It doesn't have to be there,' he said harshly. 'We can overcome it.'

She loved him for his stubborn belief. She would have given anything to yield to it and it broke her heart to refuse, knowing that she was breaking his heart in the process.

She remembered how he'd raced to the airport to stop her leaving, caring nothing for her guilt or innocence as long as he kept her with him. Surely that was enough? But he was an acquisitive man. What was his had to remain his. There might be no more in his possessiveness than that. It wasn't enough to build on.

If only, she thought desperately, there was still something that could happen—something that could give them hope for the future—but the last chance had gone. He had the evidence in his hands now, and evidence made blind trust unnecessary.

It was too late. Nothing could happen now.

'You're saying that I've failed you,' he grated. 'You can't forgive me.'

'There's nothing to forgive,' she said passionately. 'What was done to you was terrible, and it's not your fault that it's scarred you. But it has. You can't really believe in anyone now, even me. I thought I could help you but I can't. Please try to understand.'

A dead look came into his eyes.

'Yes,' he said at last. 'Of course you must go, because I let you down, didn't I? Get out while you can. Get out before I destroy you as I did her.'

He dressed hurriedly and walked out without looking back.

Shattered, she stared after him. This was what she'd planned, but now it was here it was terrible. Throwing on her clothes, she hurried out after him.

As soon as she reached the head of the stairs she knew that something had happened. The door to the cellar stood open. Through it she could see a light and hear voices.

She knew who would be there before she entered. Lysandros stood by the far wall, his eyes fixed on Nikator, who aimed a small pistol at him.

'Get out,' Lysandros shouted to her. 'Go now.'

'Oh, I don't think so,' Nikator said, pointing the pistol at her. 'I've waited so long to get you both together. Come down, my dear, and let's all three have a talk.'

She'd thought she knew the worst of Nikator. But now his eyes were bright as if he was high on something and his most dreadful side was on display. This man could kill, she was sure of it. And now only one thing mattered.

'How do you come to be here, Nikki?' she asked, trying to sound casual.

'It wasn't hard. I knew you'd both arrive soon.'

'Let her go,' Lysandros said. 'I'm the one you want.'

'But she's also the one I want. She always has been. And now I'm tired of waiting. If not one way, then another. Isn't that so?'

'Then you can have me,' Petra said. 'Let Lysandros go and I'm all yours, Nikki.'

'*No!*' Lysandros's howl of rage and despair seemed to hit the ceiling, causing some dust and wood flakes to float down.

'It makes no difference to you,' she told him, smiling. 'We'd decided to part anyway. I never stay with any man for long. What do you say, Nikki?'

She was still on the stairs and he reached up to take her hand and draw her down beside him.

'You mean you'd stay with me—?'

'If you let Lysandros go.'

Nikator laughed softly, horribly.

'Oh, darling, I so much want to believe you, but you're lying. You're still in love with him. After all the things I've heard you say to him—'

'You mean—?'

'Yes, I heard it all. It's not just the gardens that are bugged. Everywhere. I bugged it years ago. Years and years I've been waiting. I've been with the two of you all the time.'

Lysandros's roar filled the air. The next moment he'd launched himself onto Nikator. There was an explosion as the pistol went off and the next moment the whole place was shaking as the bullet hit the old ceiling, which began to disintegrate.

'It's coming down,' Lysandros said hoarsely. 'Get out fast.'

But the wooden stairs were collapsing and the next moment the ceiling began to descend on them. She saw it getting closer, then it was blocked out by Lysandros's head, and then there was darkness.

He was in the place that had always been waiting for him. Before him stretched the Styx, the river that ran between the living and the dead. He'd known in his heart that the final choice was out of his hands, and now that he was here he would go wherever the river took him.

Had there ever been a choice? He'd seen the roof coming down on the woman he loved, and he'd lunged forward to put himself between her and danger. There had been no time to think, only the knowledge that without her life was unbearable. He would die with her, or instead of her. Either way, he was content.

He ached all over from the weight of the ceiling on his

back, pinning him against her as she lay beneath him, so frighteningly still that he feared the worst.

'Not yet,' he whispered. 'Wait for me, and we'll cross the river together.'

Incredibly, he sensed a tremor beneath him. Then a soft breath broke from her.

'Petra, Petra,' he said urgently. 'Are you alive? Speak to me.'

'Aaaah—' The word was so soft he hardly heard it.

'Can you hear me?'

Her eyes opened a little way, fixed on him. 'What happened?'

'The roof fell on us. We're trapped here. There's no way out unless someone up there sees what's happened.'

And nobody would, they both realised. They were underground, in a part of the house not visible from the road. They could stay here, undiscovered, for days, perhaps longer.

'You saved me,' she murmured.

'I only wish I had.'

'You took the weight of the rafters to protect me. You could have got out—'

'And live without you? Do you think I want that? It's together or nothing.'

She managed to turn her head. There were tears in her eyes. 'Darling, are you very much hurt?'

'No, but I can't move, and I can't get you out.'

They both knew that if he tried to move he would bring the rest of the place down on them both.

'Together or nothing,' she murmured.

'There's just one thing I could try,' he said.

Taking a deep breath, he gave a shout, but immediately there was an ominous sound overhead and plaster began to pour down. They clung together, seeking refuge in each other.

'Dear God!' he said. 'I neglected this place and let it get in such bad condition. This is my fault.'

'Or maybe it's my fault,' she said softly. 'I came excavating here without thinking of safety. Who knows what damage I might have done?'

'Don't try to spare me,' he said savagely. '*I* did this. *I* harmed you. *I killed you.*'

'Darling, it doesn't matter now. Just hold me.'

'For ever,' he said fiercely, managing to get his arms about her. 'And perhaps help will come in time. We must hold on to that, Petra—Petra?'

Her eyes had closed and her breathing had become faint.

'Petra! Listen to me. For pity's sake, wake up.'

But she didn't open her eyes, and he knew that the boat was waiting for her; she was embarking on the last journey, leaving him behind.

'Not yet,' he begged. 'Not until you've heard me—forgiven me. I shouldn't have doubted you—say that you understand— that it won't part us for ever—'

Once before he'd implored forgiveness from a woman as she'd begun the journey across the river, but she hadn't heard him. Her face had been implacable as she'd climbed into the boat with her child in her arms, not seeing or hearing him, never knowing of his grief and contrition.

Now it was happening a second time, unless he could find a way to prevent it.

'Forgive me,' he whispered. 'Make some sign that you forgive me—'

For he knew that without her forgiveness they could not make the final journey together. He'd betrayed their love with his mistrust; a crime that would keep them apart for all eternity and only her blessing could wipe that out.

But she was drifting beyond him, to a place he couldn't follow.

Now he understood the face of the statue, raised in despair, calling on the gods of Olympus to grant his last request, help-less, hopeless.

'Wake up,' he begged. 'Just for a moment, *please*.'

But there was only stillness and the sound of her breath-ing, growing fainter.

As he saw her slipping away Achilles lifted his face to the heavens, silently imploring,

'Take me, not her! Let her live! Take me!'

She was in another world. There was the Styx, the river that led to the underworld and from which there was no return, save as a spirit. She looked back at the earth from which she'd come, but it was too late. She had left it for ever.

Then, coming towards her across the water, she saw a boat, with a man standing in the prow. He was tall and magnificent and all the lesser creatures fell away before him, but he had no eyes for them. He was searching for something, and when he saw her his eyes brightened and his hands reached out, imploring.

Now she knew him. He was the man who had chosen to die for her, and was asking if she was ready to follow him.

'I wasn't sure you'd come,' he said. 'It could only happen if you were willing.'

'How could I be unwilling to spend my eternity with you?' she asked.

She went towards him and he lifted her into the boat.

'Eternity,' he whispered.

The boat turned and began to make its way back across the water, until it vanished.

'My darling, wake up, please!'

Slowly she opened her eyes, frowning a little. The under-world didn't look as she'd expected. It looked more like a hospital room.

'How did I get here?'

'They came in time,' Lysandros said from where he was seated beside her bed. 'Somebody heard the gun go off and raised the alarm. Rescuers got us out.'

Now she could see him more clearly. His head was bandaged and his arm was in a sling.

'How badly are you hurt?' she asked.

'Not much; it looks worse than it is. The doctor says we're both badly bruised, but no worse.'

'What about Nikator?'

'He's alive. I got a message to Homer, and he's taking him away to a special hospital where I think he'll need to stay for some time. I've told everyone it was an accident. Nobody else needs to know the truth. Never mind him. I was afraid you weren't going to come round.'

Now she remembered. He had thrown himself between her and the descending roof.

'You saved my life,' she murmured. 'You could have been killed.'

'And so could you. Do you think I'd let you go on alone? I'd have followed, wherever you went, whether you wanted me or not.'

'Of course I'd have wanted you,' she murmured. 'How could I be unwilling to spend my eternity with you?'

'Do you mean that?' he asked anxiously. 'You spoke as though it was all over between us, and I don't blame you, but then—'

But then he had chosen to die rather than live without her. It was the sign she had longed for, his offering on the sacrificial altar. Now she belonged to him in every way, in his way, and in her own.

She had no illusions about their life together. He would

always be a troubled man, but his very troubles called on something in her that yearned to be vitally necessary to him. It would never be easy, but they belonged together.

'I'll never let you go again,' he said, 'not after that time I spent holding you down there, wondering if you were ever going to wake, whether you were going to live or die, whether you'd allow me to go with you.'

'Allow?'

'It was always up to you. You could have gone on ahead without me, or sent me on without you. I could only beg you to show me mercy. While you were unconscious I listened to the things you said, longing to hear something that gave me hope. But your words were strange and confusing.'

'Tell me about them.'

'Once you said, "The story is wrong." What did you mean?'

'The story about Achilles forcing Polyxena to die. He didn't force her. He only asked her to follow him if she was willing. And she was.'

'How do you know?'

'Never mind. I know.'

'Is this another triumphant "find" that will boost your reputation?' he asked tenderly.

'No, I'll never tell anyone else but you. This is our secret.'

He reached out a hand to touch her face with tentative fingers.

'Never leave me,' he said. 'You are my life. I can have no other and I want no other.'

'I'm yours for as long as you need me,' she vowed.

It was a few days before they were both well enough to leave the hospital. They paid a final visit to the villa and wandered through the grounds.

'I'm having it demolished,' he said. 'I could never come here again. We'll make our home somewhere else.'

'What about Brigitta, and your child? We can't leave them here. Let's take them back to Athens and let them rest in the grounds there.'

'You wouldn't mind that?' he asked.

She shook her head. 'She's part of your life, and but for her we might never have met.'

'And if we hadn't met my life would have gone on in the old dead, hopeless way. I have so much to be grateful for. I feared love as a weakness, but I was wrong. Love is strength, and the true weakling is the man who can't love, or the one who fears to let himself love.

'For years I've held myself behind doors that were bolted and barred, refusing to allow anyone through. I thought I was safe from invasion, but in truth I was destroying myself from within. Now I know that there's no true strength except what you give me in your arms, and in your heart.'

She took his face between her hands.

'You're right,' she said. 'It's not a weakness to need people. It's only a weakness if you don't know that you need them, so you don't reach out to them, and you're left floundering alone. But if you reach out, and they reach back, then your strength can defeat worlds.'

'And you did reach back, didn't you?' he asked. 'It wasn't just chance that we met again after so many years.'

'True. I think the ancient gods gave their orders from Mount Olympus.'

'And that's why it's been inevitable between us from the start—if you really feel you can put up with me.'

'How could I disobey the orders of the gods?' she asked him tenderly.

And what the gods ordered, they would protect. Their life together had been ordained, and so it must be. It would be a life of passion and pain, quarrels, reconciliations, heartbreak and joy. But never for one moment would they doubt that they were treading the path that had been preordained for them.

One day the River Styx would be waiting to carry them on, to Eternity.

But that day was not yet.

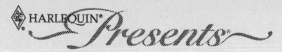
HARLEQUIN *Presents*

Coming Next Month

in **Harlequin Presents®**. Available June 29, 2010.

Coming Next Month

in **Harlequin Presents® EXTRA.** Available July 13, 2010.

LARGER-PRINT BOOKS!

GET 2 FREE LARGER-PRINT
NOVELS PLUS 2 FREE GIFTS!

YES! Please send me 2 FREE LARGER-PRINT Harlequin Presents® novels and my 2 FREE gifts (gifts are worth about $10). After receiving them, if I don't wish to receive any more books, I can return the shipping statement marked "cancel". If I don't cancel, I will receive 6 brand-new novels every month and be billed just $4.55 per book in the U.S. or $5.24 per book in Canada. That's a saving of at least 13% off the cover price! It's quite a bargain! Shipping and handling is just 50¢ per book.* I understand that accepting the 2 free books and gifts places me under no obligation to buy anything. I can always return a shipment and cancel at any time. Even if I never buy another book, the two free books and gifts are mine to keep forever.

176/376 HDN E5NG

Name _____ (PLEASE PRINT)

Address _____ Apt. #

City _____ State/Prov. _____ Zip/Postal Code

Signature (if under 18, a parent or guardian must sign)

Mail to the **Harlequin Reader Service:**
IN U.S.A.: P.O. Box 1867, Buffalo, NY 14240-1867
IN CANADA: P.O. Box 609, Fort Erie, Ontario L2A 5X3

Not valid for current subscribers to Harlequin Presents Larger-Print books.

**Are you a subscriber to Harlequin Presents books
and want to receive the larger-print edition?
Call 1-800-873-8635 today!**

* Terms and prices subject to change without notice. Prices do not include applicable taxes. Sales tax applicable in N.Y. Canadian residents will be charged applicable provincial taxes and GST. Offer not valid in Quebec. This offer is limited to one order per household. All orders subject to approval. Credit or debit balances in a customer's account(s) may be offset by any other outstanding balance owed by or to the customer. Please allow 4 to 6 weeks for delivery. Offer available while quantities last.

Your Privacy: Harlequin Books is committed to protecting your privacy. Our Privacy Policy is available online at www.eHarlequin.com or upon request from the Reader Service. From time to time we make our lists of customers available to reputable third parties who may have a product or service of interest to you. If you would prefer we not share your name and address, please check here. ☐

Help us get it right—We strive for accurate, respectful and relevant communications. To clarify or modify your communication preferences, visit us at www.ReaderService.com/consumerchoice.

HPLP10R

HARLEQUIN®

A Romance

FOR EVERY MOOD™

Spotlight on

Heart & Home

Heartwarming romances
where love can happen
right when you least expect it.

See the next page to enjoy a sneak peek
from Silhouette Special Edition®,
a Heart and Home series.

Introducing McFARLANE'S PERFECT BRIDE
by USA TODAY *bestselling author Christine Rimmer,*
from Silhouette Special Edition®.

Entranced. Captivated. Enchanted.

Connor sat across the table from Tori Jones and couldn't help thinking that those words exactly described what effect the small-town schoolteacher had on him. He might as well stop trying to tell himself he wasn't interested. He was powerfully drawn to her.

Clearly, he should have dated more when he was younger.

There had been a couple of other women since Jennifer had walked out on him. But he had never been entranced. Or captivated. Or enchanted.

Until now.

He wanted her—*her,* Tori Jones, in particular. Not just someone suitably attractive and well-bred, as Jennifer had been. Not just someone sophisticated, sexually exciting and discreet, which pretty much described the two women he'd dated after his marriage crashed and burned.

It came to him that he…he *liked* this woman. And that was new to him. He liked her quick wit, her wisdom and her big heart. He liked the passion in her voice when she talked about things she believed in.

He liked *her.* And suddenly it mattered all out of proportion that she might like him, too.

Was he losing it? He couldn't help but wonder. Was he cracking under the strain—of the soured economy, the McFarlane House setbacks, his divorce, the scary changes in his son? Of the changes he'd decided he needed to make in his life and himself?

Strangely, right then, on his first date with Tori Jones, he didn't care if he just might be going over the edge. He was having a great time—having *fun*, of all things—and he didn't want it to end.

Is Connor finally able to admit his feelings to Tori, and are they reciprocated?
Find out in McFARLANE'S PERFECT BRIDE
by USA TODAY bestselling author Christine Rimmer.
Available July 2010,
only from Silhouette Special Edition®.

Bestselling Harlequin Presents® author

Penny Jordan

brings you an exciting new trilogy…

Needed:
THE WORLD'S MOST
ELIGIBLE
BILLIONAIRES

Three penniless sisters:
how far will they go to save the ones they love?

Lizzie, Charley and Ruby refuse to drown in their debts.
And three of the richest, most ruthless men in the world
are about to enter their lives. Pure, proud but penniless,
how far will these sisters go to save the ones they love?

Look out for

Lizzie's story—**THE WEALTHY GREEK'S
CONTRACT WIFE, July**

Charley's story—**THE ITALIAN DUKE'S
VIRGIN MISTRESS, August**

Ruby's story—**MARRIAGE: TO CLAIM HIS TWINS,
September**

www.eHarlequin.com

HP12927

HARLEQUIN®

Showcase

LESLIE KELLY
Naturally Naughty

Wicked & Willing

On sale june 8

Reader favorites from the most talented voices in romance

Save $1.00 on the purchase of 1 or more Harlequin® Showcase books.

- -

SAVE $1.00 on the purchase of 1 or more Harlequin® Showcase books.

Coupon expires November 30, 2010. Redeemable at participating retail outlets.
Limit one coupon per customer. Valid in the U.S.A. and Canada only.

Canadian Retailers: Harlequin Enterprises Limited will pay the face value of this coupon plus 10.25¢ if submitted by customer for this product only. Any other use constitutes fraud. Coupon is nonassignable. Void if taxed, prohibited or restricted by law. Consumer must pay any government taxes. Void if copied. Nielsen Clearing House ("NCH") customers submit coupons and proof of sales to Harlequin Enterprises Limited, P.O. Box 3000, Saint John, NB E2L 4L3, Canada. Non-NCH retailer—for reimbursement submit coupons and proof of sales directly to Harlequin Enterprises Limited, Retail Marketing Department, 225 Duncan Mill Rd., Don Mills, ON M3B 3K9, Canada.

52609057

U.S. Retailers: Harlequin Enterprises Limited will pay the face value of this coupon plus 8¢ if submitted by customer for this product only. Any other use constitutes fraud. Coupon is nonassignable. Void if taxed, prohibited or restricted by law. Consumer must pay any government taxes. Void if copied. For reimbursement submit coupons and proof of sales directly to Harlequin Enterprises Limited, P.O. Box 880478, El Paso, TX 88588-0478, U.S.A. Cash value 1/100 cents.

5 65373 00076 2   (8100)0 11654

® and TM are trademarks owned and used by the trademark owner and/or its licensee.
© 2010 Harlequin Enterprises Limited

HSCCOUP0610